# Enter the Corpse

Roger and Meg Farrell (Margaret Hamilton, the actress) again play a large part in the affairs of their friends, Antony and Jenny Maitland.

The Farrells become involved, willy-nilly, in the concerns of Roger's godfather, who last appeared before the public in *Enter Certain Murderers*. What looked like being merely a bore becomes a dangerous adventure, and though for a while it seems that murder is the worst of their troubles, it soon becomes obvious that it is the very least of them.

What affects Roger and Meg affects Antony and Jenny as well, and though Antony's uncle, Sir Nicholas Harding, Q.C., agrees in principle that 'Meg must not be worried', he deeply disapproves of a line of action that brings his nephew again into conflict with his old adversaries at Scotland Yard. Sir Nicholas, too, has other problems on his mind, until he, in common with other characters, is swept up in the action which leads to an exciting climax in the Farrells' cottage at Grunning's Hole.

Sara Woods's worldwide readership is constantly growing, as are the number of fans who cannot have too much of Antony Maitland.

by the same author

# ENTER
# THE
# CORPSE

## Sara Woods

*sequel to Enter Certain Murderers*
*2nd Derriming 7 years ago see p.13*

*Enter the corpse of King Henry the Sixth,*
*borne in an open coffin.*

Stage Direction
KING RICHARD III, Act I, Scene ii

**MACMILLAN**

SBN 333 15399 5

*First published 1973 by*
MACMILLAN LONDON LIMITED
*London and Basingstoke*
*Associated companies in New York*
*Dublin Melbourne Johannesburg and Madras*

*Printed in Great Britain by*
THE NORTHUMBERLAND PRESS LIMITED
*Gateshead*

Any work of fiction whose characters were of uniform excellence would rightly be condemned—by that fact if by no other—as being incredibly dull. Therefore no excuse can be considered necessary for the villainy or folly of the people appearing in this book. It seems extremely unlikely that any one of them should resemble a real person, alive or dead. Any such resemblance is completely unintentional and without malice.

S.W.

3 yrs after Knives Have Edges

## Wednesday, 15th April

### I

'I really think, darling,' said Meg Hamilton, dropping her voice and looking at her companion with wide, anxious eyes, 'it's time you did something about Roger.' And Antony Maitland, who had known her for fifteen years and ordinarily discounted at least half of her histrionics, had an uncomfortable feeling that this time behind her play-acting there lay a modicum of genuine anxiety.

Not that he was going to admit this. He said, *'What about Roger?'* in a bracing tone, and turned to signal to the waiter, who was new to Astroff's, and who seemed to have perfected the art of not seeing those customers who were most in need of his services.

Meg, who had no intention of being denied her drama, wilted visibly and said in a reproachful tone, 'I should have thought you could have seen for yourself that he's worried.'

It occurred to Maitland that he might be glad before long of something sustaining in the way of drinks. He therefore ordered a double Black Label, along with the Dubonnet that he knew from experience would be Meg's choice, and then gave her again his serious attention. 'I haven't seen him for a day or two ... not since last Friday, now I come to think of it.'

'Well, didn't you think *that* was queer?' Meg demanded tartly, abandoning her drooping air and sitting up suddenly very straight indeed. The years had really changed her very little, he thought; she was small and slightly built, and she still wore her dark hair twisted round her head in a long plait, as she had done when he first saw her. Such changes as there were were more subtle. Her forthright nature was well hidden now, except from the most discerning eye, and she had learned to dress so elegantly that you very rarely noticed what she was wearing.

'As a matter of fact—' said Maitland, temporising.

'I suppose you're going to tell me you've been busy,' said Meg scathingly.

'It happens to be true.'

'All the same—'

'I did wonder,' Antony admitted. Roger Farrell, Meg's husband, was in the habit of dropping in quite frequently on the Maitlands after he had left her at the Cornmarket Theatre, where she was at the moment playing the lead in *Five for a Farthing*. 'But then I thought, a hundred things might have happened to prevent him.'

'It's worse than I thought,' Meg declared tragically. Her attention was distracted for a moment by the waiter, commendably swift once his interest had been engaged, who delivered their drinks with something of a flourish, but when the man had gone she went on as if there had been no interruption, 'I expect he's ashamed to tell you.'

'Come off it, Meg! What on earth has Roger got to be ashamed about?' She did not answer immediately, but sat looking at him sombrely, so that after a while he became uneasy and added, 'If it's something he doesn't want me to know about, hadn't we better forget the whole thing?'

'It isn't a secret,' said Meg. 'You're bound to know about it anyway, after tomorrow.'

'Tomorrow? What happens tomorrow?' His impatience was a measure of his own growing concern.

'Uncle Hubert comes out of prison.'

'Does he, though?' Maitland was startled. 'Well, but, Meg, there's nothing for you to worry about. He can't do Roger any harm, and I don't for a moment believe that Roger thinks he can. For one thing he must be—he must be well over eighty by now.'

'If you want to be exact, he'll be eighty in three months' time. I don't see what difference that makes,' said Meg.

'Doesn't it? I should have thought ... after all, what can he do?'

6

'I can tell you one thing,' she retorted. 'He's coming to stay with us.'

'*What?* Oh, no!' He stared at her, and then added, with the humour that was never very far below the surface of his thoughts, 'You've got to hand it to the old boy, he's got nerve enough for anything.'

'I didn't think you'd laugh at me,' said Meg.

'I'm not laughing.' This was not quite accurate.

'I agree that he has nerve enough for *anything*,' said Meg, unappeased.

'Yes, but even so, how did Roger come to say that he could come to you?'

'Uncle Hubert wrote to him, and the letter upset him frightfully. He went very quiet for two whole days ... you know how he does, darling; not often, but when anything really worries him. Then he snapped out of it, and even laughed when he told me he'd written to refuse, though I can't see anything funny about it myself. But that's men all over.'

'The thing is, Meg,' said Antony apologetically, 'I can't quite imagine what you'll find to talk about, over the dinner table, for instance.'

'That's just it,' said Meg, seizing on this remark and turning it to her own purposes. 'After all, Uncle Hubert tried to kill Roger, and you too.'

'So he did,' said Antony, who did not actually need to be reminded of the fact. But his tone wasn't quite solemn enough for Meg, who turned her eyes accusingly on the glass in his hand.

'I can't think it is good for you,' she told him, 'to drink at all hours of the day.'

'I'm not in court this afternoon.'

'Then I expect you have a conference in chambers,' said Meg, whom Antony had once accused of having an ambition to play Portia. 'Do you really think it's fair to your client to go in reeking of spirits?'

This time Maitland laughed aloud. He was a tall man, dark, with a thin, intelligent face and a humorous look about his eyes and mouth. 'You must admit, Meg, I need something stronger than water to cope with this story of yours,' he pleaded.

'But you didn't know what I was going to tell you when you ordered it,' said Meg prudishly.

'I knew as soon as you phoned me this morning—' But there was no need to elaborate on that. 'Let's forget my bad habits and get back to Uncle Hubert again,' he suggested.

'He isn't really Roger's uncle, he's his godfather.'

'I remember that. We'd got to the point where Roger had written to refuse his request,' he encouraged her, when she did not immediately take up her tale.

'Yes, well, you see, I thought that was that,' said Meg. 'I wasn't actually afraid he'd try to hurt Roger again; I mean, what would be the point? But about four days later the prison chaplain came to see us.'

'I'm beginning to understand.'

'I thought you might. After all, you know Roger nearly as well as I do.'

Maitland privately thought that perhaps he knew him better, but wisely he did not say so. Instead, 'You'd better tell me exactly,' he prompted.

'He was very earnest, and talked about Christian charity and the beauty of a spiritual relationship. I didn't like him much,' said Meg unnecessarily. 'And he said—of course!— that Uncle Hubert was a reformed character, and had nowhere else to go, and that it would be bad for him to be alone. And the long and the short of it was that Roger agreed—'

'Don't tell me he did so without consulting you.'

'No, of course he asked me. But what could I say, darling? I could see he was going to have a fit of conscience about it if we refused. So I said, just for a week or two, and we'd help him find somewhere to live. But I wish Roger had told you, Antony,' said Meg, with all her airs momentarily laid aside, 'because that would mean he'd got back to normal again.'

No need to ask her what she meant. Roger Farrell, who was a forceful personality and might have sat any day for the portrait of a pirate, had an odd streak of sensitivity as well; which meant that he had taken hardly certain unpalatable facts about his father which Hubert Denning had been instrumental in pointing out to him. All that had seemed to be put aside when he married Meg, even Uncle Hubert's trial not causing too bad a relapse. 'What do you think I can do about it?' Maitland wondered.

'You can talk some sense into him ... perhaps.'

'If he doesn't mean to confide in me ... are you going to tell him you've seen me?'

'I think ... on the whole, darling, I think not,' said Meg, looking down at her glass and avoiding his eye. 'You do understand, don't you?'

'You're trying to manage him, Meg. It won't do.'

'No, because ... he's been putting it off, but he's bound to tell you tonight. I just thought it would be a good idea to—to warn you, then you could be thinking what to say.'

'About this mad idea of taking in Uncle Hubert?'

'I don't think there's anything to be done about that. I meant, about the way he feels.'

'He'll get over it, Meg. He did before.'

'It's all very well to *say* that. I didn't think you'd be so unsympathetic, darling.' Meg's tone became blatantly coaxing. 'Besides that isn't ... exactly ... all.'

'I see.'

'No, you don't. I don't see how you can. And do you think—do you really think Uncle Hubert means to turn over a new leaf?'

'At eighty!'

'I don't see what difference that makes. I think if people are wicked to begin with they just get wickeder as they get older.'

'You may be right, but—'

'He's perfectly *well*. The chaplain said so. He seemed to think it was a point in his favour.'

'I told you, Meg ... he has no motive for harming Roger now.'

She hesitated perceptibly before she replied, and again she was fiddling with her glass, not looking at him. 'I do agree with you, darling, I agree with you absolutely. But indirectly ... supposing he means to—to take up his criminal activities where he left off?'

He looked at his empty glass (Meg was right, it wouldn't do to order another), and set himself to reassure her. 'Even if he wanted to, it wouldn't be practicable,' he said, but she interrupted him before he could get any further, saying fiercely,

'His age hasn't anything to do with it! He never did anything active, just organised other people.'

'That's exactly what I was going to say. His gang are scattered, some of them still in prison. How do you suppose he would go about getting them together again? Besides, the system he worked before wouldn't go down a second time.'

Meg was frowning at him. 'I don't quite know what you mean.'

'Think about it,' he instructed her, but he might have known the rather dictatorial tone wouldn't go down well.

'I haven't any data,' she flashed at him.

'Then I'd better remind you.' But his tone was conciliatory now. 'He was behind a series of spectacular bullion robberies, which puzzled the police because there was never any trace between whiles of the operatives who carried them out. A lot of blooming ghosts, Chief Inspector Sykes called them, but that was before he knew how the trick was worked.'

'I remember all that,' muttered Meg mutinously, but Maitland was well launched now and took no notice.

'Uncle Hubert owned a large, ocean-going yacht, the *Susannah*. The crew were carefully picked, for other qualities than seamanship, it made a perfect cover for them between jobs, and the proceeds of the robberies could be shipped as ballast and disposed of abroad. That's how he

10

was nailed finally ... they found the proceeds of the most recent robbery on board after the *Susannah* sank.'

'After you and Roger sank her,' Meg corrected him waspishly, and looked affronted when he smiled at her. 'Well, you did,' she insisted.

'Don't be spiteful, *darling*,' he adjured her. There was an edge on his voice, and Meg was immediately contrite. 'I know if you hadn't Roger would be dead,' she admitted. 'That was a horrible night.'

'I didn't enjoy it much myself,' said Antony, accepting the olive branch. 'But I know you and Jenny had the worst of it.'

'Yes, well, never mind that. I see what you mean about the gang, of course, but I still don't feel at all happy about Uncle Hubert.'

He was uneasy himself, but the feeling was illogical and he wasn't going to let her see it. 'Don't tell me you've got the second sight,' he said lightly.

'Have I ever claimed that?' But her next words went half way to contradict her scornful tone. 'No, really, darling, I have the strongest presentiment—'

'What do you want me to do about it?'

'Well, first of all you can tell Roger he's being silly if he starts brooding,' said Meg. Once get her to the point, Maitland reflected, and she would be as forthright as you pleased. 'Then if anything happens—'

'Nothing will.'

'You don't know that, Antony. If it does, if there's any trouble, I'd like to know you'd be standing by.'

'Heaven and earth!' said Maitland, goaded at last into a show of emotion. 'Have you dragged me here just to tell me that?'

'But, darling—'

'You know perfectly well.'

'Of course I do, but you don't know how comforting it is, just to hear you say it.'

'I can't imagine why. For one thing, I haven't actually said anything. And if it comes to that, I've got Roger into

11

more scrapes than I've ever got him out of.'

But Meg had won her point, and was not disposed to argue any further. She smiled at him sunnily, finished her Dubonnet, and said in her most dulcet tone,

'Do you mean to starve me, darling? I'm famished.'

It was no use trying to swim against the tide. Antony gave in with what grace he might, and escorted her into the dining-room.

## II

Antony and Jenny Maitland had a flat at the top of Sir Nicholas Harding's house in Kempenfeldt Square. Sir Nicholas was Antony's uncle, as well as the head of the chambers in the Inner Temple to which he belonged, and the arrangement, which in the first place had been made temporarily, had proved in so many ways a convenient one that none of them had ever seriously considered changing it. Antony was thoughtful when he went home that evening, and Jenny, who had a serenity of temperament that years of married life had so far been unable to shake, wisely did not question him. If it was anything important, he'd tell her about it soon enough.

They were having their coffee by the fire when Roger Farrell arrived, a little later than usual. He looked cold, and said he had taken Meg to the theatre by taxi, and walked from there. Jenny fussed over his comfort gently, telling him to pull his chair up to the fire, and offering to fetch another cup. Antony, for once the more practical of the two, poured whisky generously, and came back to stand on the hearth-rug looking down at his friend.

Farrell was a year or so the younger of the two men and sturdily built, so that he looked shorter than Antony, though this was an illusion. He had thick, straight, sandy-coloured hair, eyes that were vividly blue, and a stubborn line to his jaw. Now he took the glass, looked from one to the other of his companions, and said without preamble,

'I seem to have made a fool of myself.'

Maitland turned a little, to lean his shoulder against the high mantel. 'That's easily done,' he said negligently. Jenny said nothing at all, but Roger was looking at her when he spoke again. Antony followed his glance and saw the lamplight burnishing her brown curls, her grey eyes intent and a little worried, her hands clasped loosely together on her lap, and reflected, as he had so often done before, that if it wasn't for her tranquillity ...

But he hadn't time to pursue the thought. 'You may remember it's seven years since Uncle Hubert went to prison,' Roger was saying. 'He's coming out tomorrow.'

'Is he though?' said Antony. Jenny flashed him a look and asked, before Roger could speak again,

'How does that affect you?'

'I've offered to put him up for the time being, until he's found somewhere to live.'

Jenny didn't waste her time protesting. 'What does Meg say about that?' she wanted to know.

'She agreed. I don't quite know why, because I'm sure she thinks I'm mad.'

'She may be right about that,' said Maitland carefully. 'If you don't mind my asking ... why?'

'Because ... I don't know ... the padre came to see me.' This disjointed speech was about as uncharacteristic as could be of Farrell's usual directness. 'If he's right, and the old boy's really reformed ... he's eighty, you know. And there was a time—it's a long time ago now, somehow we never got along after I grew up—but there was a time when I was fond of him.'

'If you've thought better of it, find him a room at an hotel; that really might be the best thing,' said Jenny.

'That might be the most sensible thing, certainly.' Roger smiled at her wryly. 'I find this quite impossible to explain to Meg, which is odd because she's good at understanding things, but it seems to be something I have to do. And I did give my word.'

'You said, until he's found somewhere to live,' Antony

13

reminded him. 'Concentrate your energies on finding some-where, see him installed, and forget the whole thing,' he advised.

'Yes, that's easy to *say*,' Roger retorted. He meant the forgetting part, but Maitland deliberately misunderstood him.

'I know it isn't easy to find accommodation, but it isn't impossible. How is he for money, do you know?'

'All right, I should think. It would only be the actual proceeds of the robberies that were confiscated, wouldn't it? And if I know anything about it he'll have a Swiss bank account, or something like that. But the thing is ... you haven't had time to think about it yet, either of you; it's so confoundedly *awkward*,' Farrel complained. Antony began to laugh, partly at this echo of his conversation with Meg, and after a moment Roger joined in, though rather half-heartedly. 'Think of the last time we met,' he protested.

'I am doing,' said Antony. 'But you can be sure of one thing: Uncle Hubert will carry the situation off with a high hand.'

'Well, I don't want to think about it,' Jenny said, looking round the big, shabby, comfortable room almost with dislike, remembering the evening she and Meg had spent there, waiting. 'Get me a drink, Antony, and then come and sit down, and we'll look at the advertisements in the evening paper.'

The two men exchanged a look. 'Yes, I suppose that would be a good idea,' said Roger meekly. It wasn't very often Jenny took charge of things, she was more of a listener really, but when she did there was nothing for it but to fall in with her wishes.

## III

When he went downstairs to see Roger out, Maitland lingered for a moment on the doorstep, in spite of the cold. It was a clear night, with stars, but it was not any pleasure in this that held him. He was tempted to go straight up to his own quarters again, ignoring the fact that a light was still burning in Sir Nicholas's study. But it was likely to cause less commotion in the long run if he told him now of Uncle Hubert's impending release; even preoccupied with a brief, as the older man had been when he saw him that afternoon, he was not likely to remain in ignorance of the fact for long.

There was only one lamp burning in the study, its light directed on the pages of the book Sir Nicholas was holding. He laid the book down, open, as his nephew came in, smiled at him vaguely, and said, 'Good evening,' as politely as if to a stranger. 'It's getting late,' he added, as Antony crossed the room and took possession of the hearth-rug.

'Roger has just left us.' Now it came to the point he was oddly unwilling to go on. 'Do you remember Hubert Denning, Uncle Nick?'

'Denning? Denning?' said Sir Nicholas, looking rather as if he was going mad. 'I don't remember him,' he added unnecessarily.

Antony sighed. 'Seven years ago. When Roger was accused of murdering Martin Grainger.'

'I remember *that*. The man was a blackmailer.' The effort of recollection seemed to have an adverse effect on his temper and he went on gently, 'You involved me in the affair, and with your habitual carelessness left me under the impression that Roger was guilty.'

'It wasn't for want of telling you,' said Antony; but Sir Nicholas was following his own train of thought, and chose to ignore the remark.

'You got involved with Hubert Denning in the course of preparing the defence,' he said reminiscently. 'He was a relative of some kind of Roger's, I seem to recollect.'

'His godfather.'

'Ah, yes. Unfortunate.'

'Well, it was.' A certain doggedness had crept into Maitland's tone; he could not flatter himself that he was holding his learned relative's attention. 'What he was actually tried for was his part in some bullion robberies, they found the proceeds of one of them on board his yacht.'

'I suppose, my dear boy,' said Sir Nicholas cordially, 'that you have some purpose in rehearsing this rather ancient history.'

'He's coming out of prison tomorrow.'

'Need that concern us? Now if you could tell me,' said Sir Nicholas, with more vigour, 'what was the last date on which somebody was tried in this country for taking part in a duel—'

'What the devil do you want to know that for?' asked Maitland, startled out of his own preoccupation.

'The brief I'm studying—'

'Someone's been fighting a duel?'

'If you would only listen,' Sir Nicholas complained. 'My client, and—of course—the man he killed.'

'Where did this happen? And what were the weapons?'

'Do you never read the newspapers? Pistols at ten paces,' said Sir Nicholas, not without relish, 'and the incident occurred on Putney Heath. As a traditionalist I must approve the choice of venue, but I cannot find much to encourage me—'

'Uncle Nick!'

'Presently, Antony, presently. A plea of manslaughter would not be accepted, in view of the obvious premeditation. On the other hand, it seems to have been the dead man who issued the challenge. I must make what I can of that.'

'Are you pulling my leg?' Maitland demanded.

'If you mean, am I making you the object of a pleasantry,' said Sir Nicholas, pained, 'I can only say, I am not.'

'Well, of course, it's very interesting—'

'You have some communication you wish to make to me,' said Sir Nicholas, with a sudden air of alert intelligence.

'I told you, sir—'

'That a man in whom neither of us has any conceivable interest is coming out of prison tomorrow.'

16

'Roger is interested, so is Meg. He's going to stay with them.'

'Now that,' said Sir Nicholas, coming bolt upright in his chair and speaking with more energy than an observer would have thought possible a moment before, 'is absolutely absurd!' He was a man whom the newspapers habitually referred to as handsome, and perhaps the designation was not too far-fetched. He was as tall as his nephew, but much more heavily built, had fair hair—fair enough to conceal the fact that it was greying—and an authoritative manner, of which he was quite unconscious.

'All the same—' said Antony, pushing out the remark tentatively, as though it was a pawn he was putting in jeopardy.

'They must be out of their minds, the pair of them.' Having long ago accepted Meg and Roger as honorary members of his family, Sir Nicholas felt at liberty to abuse them when he felt so inclined.

'That isn't really helpful, Uncle Nick.'

'I'm not trying to be helpful, I want to know ... why?'

'I don't think I can make it sound reasonable,' said Antony cautiously. 'Roger has a sort of left-over guilt complex—'

'Spare me the psychology!'

'—because of what his father did.'

'I never had the privilege of knowing either of his parents,' said Sir Nicholas, as though that ended the matter. But to his nephew it was obviously a request for enlightenment. Antony, remembering an uncomfortable half hour which he had spent trying to explain to an unsympathetic audience the events that had led to the wreck of the *Susannah*, remembered too that he had not at that time stressed too greatly James Farrell's part in the affair. 'He knew about some of the more dubious of Uncle Hubert's activities, and kept quiet because he was afraid to talk,' he said. And then, 'Roger was fond of his father, you know.'

'A very proper sentiment.'

'Yes, I dare say.' His tone was dry, but then he added,

more naturally, 'It's all this business of remembering, Uncle Nick.'

'I should have thought that Roger, at least, had more good sense. And what is he thinking of, to expose Meg—'

'Meg agreed. She says his conscience would have plagued him if she didn't. Besides, the prison chaplain says Uncle Hubert has abandoned all his errors.'

Sir Nicholas didn't seem to think much of this. *'Are you so grossly ignorant of human nature,'* he enquired, *'as not to know that a man may be very sincere in good principles, without having good practice?'*

'As a matter of fact, I shouldn't think he's sincere at all, but after all he's getting on.' He smiled suddenly, thinking of the perfect reply to his uncle's quotation. *'At seventy-seven—and still more at nearly eighty—it is time to be in earnest.'*

'Is he to be a permanent addition to their *ménage*?'

'Good heavens, no. Just until they find him somewhere to live. I gather there's no difficulty about money.'

'Then perhaps no permanent harm will be done. I cannot approve the arrangement,' said Sir Nicholas, 'but it is after all, as you are no doubt about to remind me, no direct concern of mine.'

'The thing is, Meg's been consulting her crystal ball. She's convinced something dreadful is going to happen.'

'If you're telling me the truth—'

'I am. So far as I know it,' he added cautiously, but his uncle swept on without noticing the interruption.

'—that is surely unlikely. It would not, however, be the first time that listening to Meg has involved you in trouble.'

'N-no,' said Maitland. He sounded doubtful. 'Well, Uncle Nick, I'll leave you to your book. I just thought you ought to know what's going on.'

'I appreciate your consideration, of course,' said Sir Nicholas in a honeyed tone. But the book on his knee remained open at the same page for quite five minutes after his nephew had left him.

## IV

Jenny was still in the living-room when he went upstairs, sitting in her favourite corner of the sofa and watching the dying fire. 'You knew,' she said accusingly, as soon as Antony joined her, 'you knew what Roger was going to say before he said it.'

'I had lunch with Meg.'

'Oh, I see. That explains it. Did she think Roger wasn't going to tell you then?'

'No. When I told her I hadn't heard from him for a few days she was sure he'd get round to it tonight.'

'She wanted to—to warn you, I suppose,' said Jenny, hesitating over the word as Meg had done. 'I don't quite see why.'

'She said she hoped I'd talk sense to him.'

'You didn't exactly—'

'What *could* I say to him, love?'

'I don't know. And if Meg thought about it at all she must have realised—'

'That wasn't her real purpose,' said Antony, making a virtue of necessity. 'She wanted to be sure I'd stand by in case of trouble.'

'Well, of course you would. But ... what sort of trouble? I don't understand.'

'She thinks Uncle Hubert might start something again ... in the criminal line, I mean.'

'If he did, and if he was found out,' said Jenny practically, 'that would solve the problem, wouldn't it? He'd be back in prison again.'

'So he would. It's only a feeling she's got, Jenny. Not reasonable at all.'

'I can understand that. The very thought of Uncle Hubert gives me the creeps.'

'Me too,' Antony agreed. And hoped devoutly that she would never know how very true that was. But Jenny's mind had already left a subject which she recognised as unfruitful.

'I suppose,' she said, 'you've been telling Uncle Nick.'

'I thought it might be advisable.'

'What did he say?'

'Among other things, he quoted Johnson at me.'

'Oh, dear!' said Jenny, who knew a storm signal when she saw one. Antony smiled at her.

'Never mind, love. His attention was somewhat distracted by consideration of his latest brief. But at least he can't say now that I didn't tell him.'

They were in the bedroom when the telephone rang. Maitland threw down his tie, which he had just removed, and went back into the living-room to silence it with a bad grace. When he picked up the receiver it was Roger's voice that greeted him.

'Antony? I'm sorry to bother you, but can you come round here at once?'

He hadn't thought he would hear from Roger again that night, but now he felt as if he had expected the call all along. 'Where are you?' he asked.

'At home. We just got in.' As always when Roger was excited, his voice sounded preternaturally calm. 'I hate to tell you this, Antony, but there's the body of a man in the hall.'

'Dead?' said Maitland. He was trying to match the other man's coolness, but the word was uttered sharply, so that he sounded angry.

'Quite dead.' Farrell's voice seemed to recede, as though he had turned his head, and then came in again strongly. 'You wouldn't ask that if you could see him,' he said. 'He's got a dirty great knife sticking out of his chest.'

# Thursday, 16th April

## I

He had already removed his watch and left it in the bedroom. Antony turned a little, so that he could see the clock on the mantelpiece, and saw that it was already past midnight. What Roger had told him seemed to have blunted his capacity for surprise. 'I'll come, of course,' he said. And then, more urgently, 'Have you called the police?' That was a question that shouldn't have needed asking, but something in Roger's manner made him wonder...

'Not yet.' He hesitated, and Maitland was aware as if he could have seen him of an uncharacteristic uncertainty.

'Then call them at once,' he said, more decisively than he usually spoke.

'I want to talk to you first.' There was no doubt in Roger's tone now.

'If you want advice, you don't have to wait till I get there.'

'I thought perhaps you might call Inspector Sykes.'

Antony was impatient. 'You know perfectly well it has to go through the local people,' he said.

'Yes, but ... if what's happened is tied in with Uncle Hubert in any way, Sykes would understand without a lot of explanations.'

Maitland's voice sharpened again. 'Have you any reason for saying that?'

'Of course I have!'

'Who is he ... the dead man?'

'I didn't say I knew him.'

'You implied—'

'I don't know his *name*.' He'd got Roger on the defensive now. Antony waited in silence, and after a moment his friend went on, 'He's one of the chaps who kidnapped me—do you remember?—and took me aboard the *Susannah*.'

'Are you sure?'

'I wish I weren't.'

'I see.' He sounded thoughtful now. 'Even so ... what in the name of all that's wonderful is he doing in your house?'

'I hoped you might have some ideas about that.'

'I'm afraid my ingenuity is not quite equal—' He stopped, hearing in his own voice an echo of Sir Nicholas at his testiest, which wasn't going to do anything to set Roger at his ease. 'Look here, phone the police now ... right away ... immediately!'

'I heard you the first time.'

'Good. Tell them exactly what happened, I mean how you found him and all that, but don't go into any other details, if you can help it, until I get there. We can explain to them then why they ought to get in touch with Scotland Yard.'

'*You* can explain to them,' said Roger gloomily.

'If you like. The point is that there shouldn't be any further delay.'

'Understood.' But he still didn't ring off. 'Meg says she knew something awful was going to happen.'

'Tell her to stop playing Cassandra. But at least you can be thankful she isn't having hysterics,' said Maitland, confident that he knew Meg well enough to assume that. Roger gave a laugh that didn't sound to have much amusement in it, and he moved the receiver away from his ear.

'She's in the living-room, drinking brandy,' Farrell told him. 'For medicinal purposes only ... she hates the stuff.'

'I know. All this is wasting time, Roger. If I ring off now will you do exactly as I say?'

'If you think—'

'I do!'

'All right then. But for heaven's sake try and get here,'

said Roger, 'before they have time to ask too many questions.'

'I'll do that.' But he sat with his hand on the receiver for quite thirty seconds after he had replaced it. He didn't like what he had heard, and he didn't think Jenny was going to like it. There was a feeling of time returned about the whole thing. Seven years ago, when he had first met Roger, when Meg had first brought him to the house in Kempenfeldt Square...

He was lucky to find a taxi drawing away from the Royal George Hotel, round the corner in Avery Street. But the journey to Chelsea, where Meg and Roger had lived for the last couple of years, seemed interminable, and he found himself quite incapable of constructive thought. At best, the whole unpleasant business was going to be raked up again. At worst ... but how the hell could it have anything to do with Uncle Hubert, who wasn't due out of prison until the next day?

The police were already in occupation when he got to Beaton Street. There were two cars parked in the roadway, and when he rang the bell the door was opened to him by a man whom he took to be a detective-constable in plain clothes. The hall, which didn't seem over-large at the best of times, was crowded. A rather stout man, crouched uncomfortably with his back to the door, who must be the doctor; a man with photographic apparatus; two more, who looked to be in a state of suspended animation, and who might, Antony supposed vaguely, be fingerprint experts; the uniformed men from the police car, who for lack of room were grouped together on the staircase.

It seemed he was expected. The constable stood aside for him to enter, and gestured towards the living-room. 'Mr Maitland? If you'll just go in there, sir.' But first Antony had every intention of getting a good look at the cause of all the disturbance.

He could see the dead man now, over the doctor's shoulder; he was lying on his back with his legs drawn up awkwardly, as though he had crumpled slowly from a standing

23

position and then fallen backwards. The knife was very much in evidence, though smaller than he had expected from Roger's description. An upward blow, he thought, to miss the rib cage and find the heart. Certainly the man had died quickly. There was surprisingly little blood.

He had been tall in life, with a hefty pair of shoulders. Darkish hair, a jutting forehead, beetling eyebrows, and a craggy chin. Not a prepossessing face, hard even for a mother to love. His suit might have been fairly new, though not of the first quality, and his shirt had obviously been worn for several days. His tie was wide, and garishly coloured, but not spotlessly clean.

'Ever seen him before?' enquired a voice from the doorway of the living-room. Antony looked up and saw a thin, fair-haired man in plain clothes eyeing him quizzically. 'Divisional Detective Inspector Rawdon,' said the constable helpfully at his back.

They stood for a moment, each openly appraising the other, and then Antony said, 'No, he's a stranger to me,' and began to edge past the body. The detective backed away from the doorway and motioned to him to enter. He was aware that the constable followed him in, produced a notebook, and seated himself unobtrusively in a corner.

For an instant the familiar room looked strange to him. Perhaps it was Meg, sitting stiffly upright in the chair at the right of the fireplace, as though she was a visitor who had forgotten the formula for saying good-night and getting herself out of the house. Roger was lounging, but he didn't look relaxed. But everything else was as usual, and Antony took some comfort from that ... even the subtly disorganised air that Farrell imparted to a room merely, it seemed, by going into it was, in the circumstances, reassuring. Somebody had been rummaging along the bookshelves with a careless hand; there was an evening paper on the floor, a vase of chrysanthemums balanced precariously on the extreme edge of a side table, gramophone records reared against the wall in no sort of order; the picture over the fireplace—a tranquil enough subject, 'A fishing village at dawn'—hanging slightly askew. Antony crossed the room to Meg's side, and she put out a hand to him. Hers was cold, and he thought not quite steady, but he noted with approval that she maintained her self-possession.

'Darling,' she said, 'I'm so glad you're here.' For once the endearment came completely naturally, without the teasing note she so often imparted to it.

Antony gave her hand a squeeze, and let it go. 'I came as quickly as I could,' he said.

'And just in time to save Inspector Rawdon's reason,' said Roger enthusiastically. 'Mr Maitland's a barrister, as well as being a friend of mine,' he added. 'He'll be able to explain much more clearly—'

'I shall be grateful to him.' Besides the formality, there was a touch of humour in the detective's tone. 'Shall we sit down, Mr Maitland?' He waited until Antony had complied with this suggestion before he went on, 'Mr Farrell assures me you know as much about the background to this affair as he does.'

'Wait a bit! I don't know as much about what happened this evening. After you left us, Roger—'

'I took a taxi round to the theatre, waited about ten minutes for Meg, and then we both came home. When we opened the door ... there he was. So I phoned you, and then I phoned the police station. Inspector Rawdon is from Lennox Street.'

'I see.' He met the detective's eye and smiled faintly. Roger's tone was matter-of-fact ... too matter-of-fact? It was difficult to know how someone he knew so well impressed other people. 'There's one other thing. How did the dead man, and whoever killed him, get into the house?'

'Not by breaking and entering.' Rawdon's tone was emphatic. 'I've been all round and there's not a sign. If he wasn't let in—'

'I've told you, Inspector, there was nobody here to do it,' said Roger, a little too quickly. 'We've no servants living in.'

'Then somebody had a key.' There was no animosity in

the detective's tone, but it was flat and didn't encourage contradiction. Maitland said into the silence that followed,

'Well, Inspector, we've got to go back seven years to the beginning of the story. Do you remember a series of bullion robberies which kept you people guessing for quite a long time?'

'I do.' Obviously this wasn't what Rawdon had been expecting. There was surprise in his tone, and a touch of hostility, as though he suspected that he was about to be made the victim of an elaborate joke.

'If I remember rightly, eleven men were tried and convicted in connection with those robberies. One of them was Hubert Denning, who owned the yacht, *Susannah*, on which the proceeds of the most recent theft were found.'

'I don't recall the details.'

'They aren't important.' He suppressed firmly his desire to get up and wander round the room; Meg wasn't one to show her feelings, except, as now, by the unnatural propriety of her attitude, but he didn't want to add to her anxiety so that it became obvious, even to a stranger. 'Hubert Denning is Farrell's godfather. It isn't important, either, how he and I came to be involved, but the night things came to a head we were—I suppose I should say trapped on board the *Susannah*, if it didn't sound so melodramatic, and only got away by starting a fire and going over the side in the confusion. The point about all this is that the crew were also the members of the gang who had been carrying out the robberies, and Farrell recognised that chap out there as one of them.'

'Indeed?' There was no doubt about Rawdon's interest now, or about his antagonism. 'One of the eleven men?'

'No.' Roger had left his lounging position, and was sitting erect. He showed no sign now that he saw anything unusual or worrying in the situation. 'I should have explained that to you, Antony. He was sent on an errand by Uncle—by Mr Denning before you arrived, and wasn't on board when the fire started.'

'Wasn't he ever arrested then?'

26

'Not that I know of. I suppose he heard what had happened and laid low until the trial was over. The police may never even have heard his name; I didn't know it, and I can't see that it would do any of the others any good to mention him.'

'The question remains, Mr Farrell, what was he doing here?'

'I haven't the faintest idea. But—'

'I hadn't quite finished, Inspector,' Antony put in. 'It doesn't make things any clearer, but it must have some bearing on the situation. Hubert Denning is coming out of prison tomorrow, and will be staying in this house for a few days at least.'

'Here?' Rawdon's voice rose on the word, perhaps in protest against the unreasonableness of the last statement.

Antony said, 'That's right,' and tried to sound as if it were the most natural thing in the world. He didn't think it did much to enlighten the inspector, and nor did Meg's gentle remark,

'There was nowhere else for him to go,' made in her saddest voice. Cordelia perhaps, thought Maitland, half exasperated, half amused.

'Well!' said Rawdon, which seemed as good a comment as any. And then, 'All the same, I don't really see—'

Antony took one look at Roger's face, and interrupted without ceremony. 'It's only the fact that really concerns you,' he pointed out.

'Well,' said the detective again. 'Yes, I suppose so,' he added doubtfully. 'But you must see, Mr Maitland, that I can't leave this—this story of yours there.'

'That's why I want to suggest that you get in touch with Scotland Yard. In the circumstances ... Chief Inspector Sykes could vouch for the truth of what I'm telling you, and fill in the details much more satisfactorily than I can.'

'It's all very irregular,' said Rawdon, shaken now to the point of indecision. 'Suppose I go along with you, suppose I agree to that? There are still questions that have to be answered.'

'Anything that Mr Farrell can do to help you,' said Antony, not looking now at his friend. Roger muttered something that might have been agreement; at any rate, Rawdon chose to take it that way.

'Well then, Mr Farrell,' he said, but he still sounded unsure of himself, 'I have to ask you whether you have had any dealings with this man—the dead man, whatever-his-name-is—since the night Mr Maitland has described to me, the night this Mr Denning was arrested, as I take it.'

'No, of course not.' Roger was definite. 'If I'd seen him again I'd have told the police.'

'And Mr Denning has not made any communication to you that might explain—'

'I tell you, I've no idea what the connection might be. The connection, I mean, between my godfather coming out of prison and that man being found dead ... here.'

'You will admit that some connection must exist?'

'It would seem so.' He looked at Antony. 'Wouldn't you agree?' Neither face nor voice had much expression, but the words managed to convey, at least to the man to whom they were addressed, a sense of almost frantic appeal.

'So long as the inspector realises that it is a matter of opinion only, on your part as on mine. We have no knowledge on which to base it.'

'Logically—' began Inspector Rawdon, and broke off when he saw that Maitland was smiling.

'You mustn't ask Mr Farrell any questions, the answers to which can only be based on conjecture,' he said; and watched with interest the detective's struggles to suppress a sharp retort.

'Very well,' Rawdon said at last. 'At least, you will perhaps allow your client to answer me this—'

'Not my client, Inspector. I'm a barrister, I thought Mr Farrell had explained that to you. If he'd felt any need for legal advice he'd have consulted his solicitor, of course.'

'Of course!' He might be forgiven if his tone was dry, but he hadn't lost his temper and that, as Maitland conceded privately, was one up to him. 'In any case, my question is a very simple one, and perhaps I had better put it first to Mrs Farrell.' He turned until he was facing Meg, and when he spoke his voice was wary. Antony didn't blame him for that; he found her unpredictable himself, at times. 'If I understand what your husband told me correctly,' said the inspector, 'you were at the *Cornmarket Theatre* last night from about seven-thirty on.'

'Me?' said Meg, for all the world as if she hadn't been listening to every word that was said. And then, with a touch of the *grande dame*, which she could assume when she chose, 'Are you really asking us for alibis, Mr Rawdon?'

The answer to that was simple. 'Yes,' said the detective, and spoiled the effect by adding, apologetically, 'In the circumstances—'

'I see.' Nothing could have exceeded Meg's condescension. 'Certainly I was at the theatre, from seven-thirty until well after half past eleven.'

'On stage most of the time?' Rawdon persisted. Meg gave him a pitying smile.

'From eight o'clock until nine ... no, we were running a little late tonight, until ten past nine,' she amended. 'And then again from nine twenty-five until nearly eleven.'

'Thank you.'

'I don't really think I could have come back here and committed a murder while I was supposed to be in my dressing-room,' said Meg thoughtfully. She didn't know what Antony's game was, but she was playing up magnificently. Rawdon was exhibiting every symptom of acute embarrassment. 'Of course, you could ask my dresser. But I assure you it takes me all my time to get my make-up on and off, and to change between the acts.'

'Yes ... yes, I'm sure. And you, Mr Farrell?' Roger's expression was forbidding, but the detective turned to him with obvious relief.

'I left my wife at the theatre ... I've told you all this before, Inspector,' said Roger stiffly. 'Then I went round to Kempenfeldt Square to visit the Maitlands; you can confirm that, Antony.'

29

'I can.'

'That's all really. I picked up a cab when I left them at about a quarter past eleven, went back to the theatre again, waited for my wife—who was ready at precisely twenty to twelve, if the information is of any interest to you—and then we came home together.'

'Did you dismiss the cab when you arrived at the theatre?'

'No. I left it at the stage door while I went to tell Meg that it was waiting. I could have gone out through the theatre, I suppose,' he went on, heavily sarcastic, 'but there would hardly have been time—'

'If that is true,' said Rawdon, reserving judgment, 'the only opportunity for you to return here would be after you left the theatre for the first time and before you arrived in Kempenfeldt Square.'

'You mustn't mind the inspector,' said Maitland, before Roger could speak. 'He's a policeman, and all policemen have suspicious minds.'

'So they have.' Roger looked at Antony for a long moment before he turned back to the detective and added, much less defensively, 'I did the journey on foot and arrived just after eight-fifteen.'

'Three quarters of an hour,' said Rawdon, making the words sound like a question.

'I wasn't in a hurry. There were things I wanted to think out.'

'What things, Mr Farrell?'

'The problem of what to do with Uncle Hubert for one thing,' said Roger. He glanced at Antony, and then back at the inspector again. 'Murdering a man almost unknown to me formed no part of the solution,' he went on.

'You had reached some conclusion then?'

'That, Inspector, is nothing to do with you.'

'I am beginning to think that anything to do with Mr Denning—'

'Mr Farrell is helping you to the best of his ability,' Maitland put in. 'You really mustn't push him too far.'

'Very well!' That was all the acknowledgement that

Rawdon made, and he did not take his eyes from Roger's face. 'There is still the period before you left the house, Mr Farrell, which you have not accounted for.'

It was Antony who answered that, saying quickly, 'Has the doctor been able to give you an estimated time of death?'

'He declined to do so.' There was no resentment in Rawdon's tone, he took the interruption stoically. 'As you know, at this stage it could only be a guess.'

'And you think ... you really think,' said Meg, coming suddenly and with great energy into the conversation, 'that we killed him and left him here dead, while we went calmly out for the evening?'

'I told you, Meg,' said Antony, alarmed by her vehemence. 'it's his job to ask questions.'

'But such questions! Ridiculous!' said Meg, regal again.

'Until the doctor has given his opinion—' said Rawdon cautiously. 'Of course, if you don't wish to answer—' He seemed incapable, for the moment, of finishing a sentence.

'Neither Mr nor Mrs Farrell has any objection, Inspector,' said Maitland, in a hurry.

'Betty, who is our daily maid, left at four o'clock,' said Meg frostily, giving Antony a look that ought to have withered him. 'I dare say you will take her word for it, when you see her, Mr Rawdon, that nothing abnormal had gone on up to that time.'

'And after four o'clock?'

'I was alone until Roger came in. I didn't notice the time, but it is usually about six.' She glanced at Roger, who nodded his assent, but he was still frowning. 'He had dinner and I had a snack at about a quarter to seven, and we went out almost immediately afterwards.'

'Nobody phoned, nobody called at the house during that time?'

'Nobody.'

'Can you tell me of any circumstance recently that might be connected with this affair?'

'No.'

31

'Mr Farrell?'

'No, Inspector.'

'There is just one other thing then ... the question of access to the house.'

Antony, who had hoped the question had been side-tracked for that night at least, took it upon himself to answer. 'Mr Farrell has already told you that there was nobody in the house during the evening.'

'There are just the two doors, aren't there ... front and back? No way into the basement?'

'The back door is usually bolted,' Meg volunteered, 'after Betty goes home.'

'That's how I found it this evening. There remains the front door,' said Rawdon, looking from one of them to the other and not attempting to conceal his distrust of any-thing they might tell him. 'How many keys are there?'

'Three,' said Roger. 'We each have one, and so has the maid.' He paused, frowning. 'Betty certainly used hers to let herself in this morning ... Meg was still in bed and I was shaving when she arrived. It doesn't seem likely that she lost it since then.'

'Well, I shall have to ask her,' the inspector began, but Meg interrupted him, saying eagerly,

'I don't see how it helps, but I lost my key at the week-end.'

'You never—' said Roger, and broke off.

This time it was Rawdon's turn to frown. He said sharply, 'Lost? Where?'

'If I knew that it wouldn't *be* lost,' said Meg, pointing out the obvious in rather a smug tone. 'And I didn't notice till Monday morning, Roger, so I borrowed Betty's key and had another one cut. I never thought to tell you ... it didn't seem important.'

'I could have arranged to have the lock changed.'

'But darling, no-one could have known it was mine. It didn't have a label on, or anything like that.'

Roger shrugged. Rawdon said, watching him, 'Mrs Farrell, where was this key usually kept?'

'In my handbag. In my change purse to be exact, so that I always had it with me, whichever one I was using.' The detective turned his eyes to her then, with something of a blank look, and she added impatiently, 'I don't always use the same handbag, you know.'

'No, I see. Who could have taken the key?'

'I don't think anyone took it. I'm always losing things.'

'Even so—'

'Mrs Farrell is tired. There will be time enough for all this tomorrow,' said Maitland, getting up. Rawdon rose as he did, and gave him an unamiable look, but rather to Antony's surprise he did not attempt to argue but only said,

'Very well,' this time in a tone that was rather resigned than otherwise.

'And in the meantime, I hope, you will talk to Chief Inspector Sykes.'

'I'll do that. But I'm afraid—'

'I know, you want to search the house. I'm proposing to take Mr and Mrs Farrell home with me—don't argue, Meg, Jenny will have got the bed made up in the spare room by this time—then they'll be out of your way.'

'That's a good idea, sir.' He was even grateful for the suggestion, which he wouldn't have been if he had known Maitland better. And when Meg, supervised by Constable Hall, had packed what they both needed for the night, he sent them back to Kempenfeldt Square in one of the police cars.

They had no conversation on the way, except that Meg said plaintively, 'I know it sounds heartless to say so, darling, but I'm starving,' and Antony replied,

'Jenny knows your habits, Meg. She'll have something ready for you.'

Roger said nothing at all.


II

Jenny was wearing a house-coat, but she had taken time

33

to brush her hair after taking off the dress she had worn during the day, and looked, in consequence, the neatest of the four of them. Even Roger, who was never tired, and who generally seemed to thrive on adversity, had a slightly jaded look. Meg, with dark circles under her eyes, might have been suffering from a hangover, if she ever took anything stronger than Dubonnet, and very little of that; a few wisps of hair had escaped from the restraining plait, and when she took off her coat her dress was rumpled ... a thing unheard of. She hugged Jenny briefly, said, 'Bless you!' and went over to the fire. Antony followed her more slowly, moving a little stiffly as he did when he was tired and his shoulder was paining him, while Roger went with Jenny into the kitchen to help with the tray.

Meg held her hands to the blaze and turned to look up at her host. She was observant, as her profession had taught her, but she knew better than to comment upon what she saw. 'If it hadn't been for you, darling,' she said, 'we might have been there all night.'

'I thought,' said Antony, joining her on the hearth-rug but not meeting her eye, 'that we could go into the question of the key together, first.'

'Shouldn't I have mentioned it?'

'No, it was the right thing to do.'

'I thought ... you *made* me answer his other questions, darling.'

'No sense in antagonising the police.'

'But before that ... you were trying to make him angry, weren't you?'

'Rightly or wrongly, I thought that was one way to persuade him to get in touch with Sykes. You played up marvellously, Meg. I can't say the same for Roger.'

She was moved to protest. 'I don't suppose you'd like it, Antony, if you came home late one night and found a corpse just inside the front door.'

'I'm not criticising, Meg. I didn't mean to. Quite rightly, he doesn't like you being involved.' The others came in then, and he bent to pull the coffee table into a more convenient position. 'Sit down and have your supper, then we can talk.'

Roger set down the tray. It was difficult to define the change in him since the police car had dropped them outside the house, but he seemed altogether more relaxed. 'I thought,' he said, and looked up and smiled as he caught Antony's eye, 'that Mr and Mrs Farrell were too tired to answer any more questions.'

'That only applied to the police inquisition, not to mine.'

'You can't bother them any more tonight,' said Jenny. Perhaps some of Roger's anxiety had rubbed off on her; her grey eyes were worried.

'Can't I, love?' said Antony. He sounded as if he really wanted an answer.

'I suppose you mean, you're glad of the chance to talk to them before there are any more questions from the police.' Jenny sat down at one end of the sofa and patted the cushion beside her invitingly. 'You may as well sit down, Roger, and get what rest you can.' Then she looked back at her husband again. 'Inspector Sykes would have known better than to give you the opportunity,' she said, and smiled at him.

'That reflection doesn't comfort me at all.'

'But Roger said you wanted—'

'Of course I did! Here we are with a preposterous story. Sykes's intervention is the only thing that can make Inspector Rawdon look on us more kindly.'

'You think it will have that effect?' asked Roger, reaching out absent-mindedly and helping himself to a sandwich.

'It can't fail. Sykes knows what happened before, and that you were only innocently involved. That's not what's worrying me.'

'What then?'

'This business ... it's insane!'

'I agree with you there,' said Roger. 'What do you think happened? This chap got hold of a key somehow ... and that reminds me, Meg—'

35

'Don't say it, darling. I ought to have told you mine was lost.'

'Well, you should.' He looked up again at Antony, who was still standing with his back to the fire. 'This chap got hold of a key somehow,' he repeated, 'and I suppose he let himself in.'

'It needn't have been like that. He might have been ringing the door-bell like any visitor and been joined by the man—or, more likely, the men—who killed him. They had a key, and one of them opened the door and they hustled him inside. *Voilà tout!*'

'And after that—?' said Meg, putting down her soup bowl and turning her attention to the plate of sandwiches and the glass of milk that Jenny had provided.

'If you want the gory details—'

'Is it very unwomanly of me? I'm afraid I do.'

'Well then, I should imagine that one of them took hold of his arms from behind and held him while the other stabbed him.' Meg made a moue of distaste. 'Neat, and quick,' said Antony, ignoring her. 'There were no signs of a struggle.'

'But why leave him there?' said Roger. 'Why not take him away and *then* kill him?'

'At a rough guess, Roger, I should say ... as a warning.'

There was a pause while Roger digested this. He said at last, 'I'm afraid I don't follow you. What could anybody want to warn me about?'

'I don't know.'

'That isn't really helpful.'

'I know. I'm sorry. If you want me to guess, Roger'—his eyes slid to Meg for a moment, assessing her possible reaction—'I'd say that possibly "they" are a group of people with whom Uncle Hubert is unpopular.'

'You mean, because I seem to be helping him—'

'It still doesn't make sense,' said Meg roundly. Roger looked at her and shook his head slightly, and then turned back to Antony again.

'What do you think I ought to do?' he demanded.

'On the odd chance that I'm right? Send the old boy to an hotel until you can find him a suitable flat.'

'But—you don't have to remind me you're guessing, Antony—might not that just be handing him over to his enemies?'

'*Je m'en fiche!*' said Antony bluntly.

'I daresay. All the same—'

'I agree with Roger,' said Meg, with rather more determination than the statement called for. 'We can't do that, not when we've promised.'

'Wouldn't it be better to wait and see what Uncle Hubert has to say about it,' Jenny suggested. They all turned and looked at her. 'He may be able to explain the whole thing,' she went on. 'After all, warning Roger can't have been the only motive for this man's death.'

'All right then.' Roger sounded relieved. 'He's due to arrive sometime tomorrow afternoon, I've told Meg I'll stay home from the office. If you'll come round in the evening, Antony—'

'I will, of course. But I still think it's a damn fool thing to take him in.'

'That's all very well, darling,' said Meg tartly. 'I wouldn't say you were always a model of good sense yourself.'

There was a hint of wryness in Antony's smile. 'Let's not quarrel,' he said pacifically. 'We'll talk to Uncle Hubert, and go on from there. Meanwhile, Inspector Rawdon, and most likely Sykes too, will be wanting to see you again tomorrow.'

'Will you be there?' asked Roger hopefully, and looked despondent when Antony shook his head.

'Better not. You've nothing to worry about, but it wouldn't be a good idea to create the impression that you need me to hold your hand.'

Meg ruffled up at the suggestion, but Roger smiled for the first time since he had left them earlier in the evening. 'There is nothing,' he said, '—is there?—like having a candid friend.'

'You may live to thank me,' Antony told him lightly.

'But what Sykes will want to know tomorrow, and what I want to know now, is what about that key?'

'What about it?'

'The man got in somehow. And the lock on your front door, as Inspector Rawdon undoubtedly noticed, is not the kind to yield to casual persuasion. If Betty can produce the key she used as lately as this morning ... yesterday morning, I mean; what about Betty, by the way? Might she have been planted on you?'

'Two years ago!'

'It doesn't sound likely, I admit, but there's always the possibility she might have been got at. If she'd lent her key to somebody, perhaps only long enough for him to have it copied—'

'I don't think much of that idea, darling,' said Meg judiciously. 'She isn't the type.'

'Is there a type ... that isn't interested in money, for instance?'

'That's very cynical, even for you, Antony. What I mean —it sounds awfully proud to say it—she likes working for *me*.'

'That's reasonable enough.'

'Thank you, darling. I meant really, for Margaret Hamilton.'

'Yes, I see. It's still possible—'

'But very unlikely.'

'All right. Leaving Betty aside for the moment, and assuming that your key has never been out of your possession, Roger—'

'It hasn't.'

'Very well then. That only leaves yours, Meg.'

'Anybody might have picked it up, darling.'

'Don't be silly. You said yourself it wasn't identifiable in any way. Somebody got hold of it who knew, or had good reason to believe, that it was the key to your house, and the only explanation of that is that it was taken from your handbag.'

'But nobody—'

38

'Don't be in too much of a hurry. Even Sykes might look askance at Roger's activities if we can't show that someone might have got into the house without his assistance.'

He thought that Meg was going to flare up again at that; not that he could blame her for being touchy, all things considered. But she only looked at him stonily for a moment, and then gave him one of her most dazzling smiles. 'You do have the nicest way of putting things, darling,' she said.

'Never mind that. When did you notice the key was missing?'

'On Monday morning. I'm always up early on Mondays, because of no theatre on Sunday night, and I was going shopping, but it wasn't there.'

'How did you know?'

'I looked in my purse, of course.'

'Do you usually do that, Meg? Check and see if you've got your key before you go out, I mean.'

'No. No, I don't. Hardly ever.'

'Then why did you do it on that particular morning?'

'I don't know. I just did.'

Antony shook his head at her. 'Don't scowl at me, *darling*. You'll give yourself wrinkles.'

'How can I help it when you ask me such stupid questions?'

'Leave it, then. When did you last have the key?'

'I don't ... oh, yes, I do know, now I think about it. I went round the corner for some cigarettes on Saturday afternoon. Betty had gone, and Roger was reading the *Financial Times,* so I just let myself in without disturbing him.'

'Wait a bit. You neither of you smoke, so why——?'

'Really, darling! We had some people coming in on Sunday evening, it's the only time we have for entertaining, you know.'

'Which handbag were you carrying?'

'This old, black thing.' The handbag, which was sharing

the wing chair with her, was as sleek and elegant as Meg generally was herself.

'And did you have occasion to change your things into another bag before Monday morning when you found the key was missing?'

'I don't ... no, of course I didn't. I was busy on Sunday with dinner, because Betty doesn't come in that day. Roger went for a walk, but I didn't go with him.'

'Now we're getting to it. I want you to account for the handbag, every minute of the time, between Saturday afternoon and Monday morning.'

'Darling, I can't possibly—'

'We were both at home until you went to the theatre that evening. No-one else was in the house,' said Roger.

'Yes, well, the bag was in my dressing-room while I was on stage, of course.'

'Would your dresser be there?'

'Millie? Most of the time, I should think. We've been running nearly a year, so she can't be interested in the play any more, and anyway she enjoys pottering.'

'In the second act,' said Roger, 'you have to make a quick change in the wings.'

'How clever of you, darling. Millie has to be there, of course, with the things I need. But unless somebody knew—'

'Anybody in the theatre would know that.'

'But why should they—?'

'Somebody might have been bribed, I suppose.' Meg shook her head violently. 'You can't *know*,' he insisted. 'For that matter, it would have been quite easy for Millie—'

'Darling, she's been with me for ten years.'

'You trust her, obviously, or else you wouldn't be employing her, but—' He broke off there and added, in a gentler tone, 'I can see you hate the idea, Meg, but we must think of everything.'

'You mean you want me to tell ... all this ... to the police.'

'Every last word of it.'

'It's so silly, darling. Why I'd as soon think—'

He smiled at her when she stopped short, staring at him. 'You were going to say, you'd as soon think one of your guests on Sunday night took the key. Weren't you?'

'It's equally stupid,' said Meg mulishly.

'Who came to the house that day?'

'Nobody, until evening.'

'You may as well tell him, Meg,' said Roger. 'Or I will, if you like. Two couples you know, Antony. Isabel and Leonard—'

'Your sister and her husband?'

'Why not? We happen to be on speaking terms at the moment,' said Roger, amused by his friend's startled tone. 'The others were Sam and Irene Reade, and Victor Barham and his daughter, Terry.' He turned to Jenny. 'Sam's my partner, in case you've forgotten.'

'And Barham?' said Antony, reclaiming his attention again.

'He's the Managing Director of the Imperial Insurance Company. He's a bit of a stuffed shirt, but we exchange visits occasionally.'

'Not, in fact, a gathering of your best friends,' said Antony, blunt again. Roger laughed.

'An evening with Isabel and Leonard is wasted anyway,' he confided. 'It's a good opportunity to get our duty entertaining taken care of at one fell swoop.'

'Darling, *don't*!' said Meg. And when they all looked at her, '*Macbeth*,' she explained tragically.

'I shouldn't worry,' Antony told her. 'He's only theatre-by-marriage, so I daresay it doesn't count.' He looked from Meg, to Roger, and back again, trying to decide which of them was the more likely to give him the information he wanted. 'Now we've only to make up our minds which of these people had the opportunity—'

'Any of them,' said Roger. 'But unless you can tell me what reason—'

'Jenny was right, we shall have to wait until we've talked to Uncle Hubert to know that. And even then we may not *know*.'

'In any case,' said Roger, pursuing his own train of thought, 'can you imagine Leonard, or Sam, or Victor for that matter ... you don't know him, but I assure you it's just as unlikely—'

'I never said, you know, that the person who stole the key committed the murder. Did you tell them about Uncle Hubert?'

'I shouldn't have done, but I'd mentioned it to Sam, at the office, and he brought the subject up. Isabel was outraged, as you might have expected.'

'Because he's coming to you?'

'That, of course. But the mere mention of his name is enough. She'll never forgive him for all the publicity.'

'It needn't have worried her. It's not as though he were actually a relative.'

'No, but their friends knew she called him Uncle. And she was rather a favourite of the old boy, you know. He appreciated her regard for the conventions.'

Jenny smiled at that. 'He doesn't seem to have had much time for them himself,' she said.

'Funnily enough, it's perfectly true,' said Roger seriously. 'He quite genuinely disapproved of me.'

'Because you got in the way of his plans.'

'Long before that,' he assured her. Jenny didn't look convinced, but Antony spoke before she had time to argue.

'Where was Meg's handbag all this time?'

'On the chest on the upstairs landing, where she always leaves the one she's using.'

'Then anyone—' Antony started, but Meg interrupted him, saying with the first approach to enthusiasm she had shown,

'That's funny. Antony, darling, you may have something there.'

'Have you gone mad too?' asked Roger in a resigned voice.

'No, this is serious. My handbag,' said Meg impressively, 'wasn't on the chest on Monday morning when I looked for it, it was on the window-ledge in the other bathroom. I mean, not the one we use.'

'I don't believe it,' said Roger, but he sounded more bewildered than anything else.

'That isn't very polite, darling. Anyway, it's true, whether you believe it or not. I think now that must have been why I looked through it, because I was a bit puzzled to find it where it was. But I never thought until this minute—'

'Are you suggesting that Sam, or Leonard, or Victor—?'

'Or Isabel, or Irene, or even Terry,' said Meg. 'One of them could have taken the handbag in there, where they could be sure of being private.'

'Were they all upstairs during the evening?'

'The women were, of course, to leave their coats. Otherwise, I just don't remember. I had other things on my mind, and they drank two pots of coffee so I wasn't even in the room all the time.' She broke off, and came down to earth with a bang. 'I can't see why any of them should have wanted the key,' she added dejectedly.

'Motive will have to wait,' said Antony, as excited as she was but more cautious about showing it. 'They all of them knew Uncle Hubert, didn't they? At least, I don't know about Barham.'

'He knew him all right,' said Roger, suddenly amused again. 'Uncle Hubert was a director of Imperial, you know. But this doesn't make sense.'

'I know.' Antony was sympathetic. But whatever he had been going to say was forestalled by Meg, who gasped dramatically and exclaimed,

'I can't ... Antony, you must see that I can't tell the police all this.'

'They'll ask you,' he pointed out.

'Yes, but—'

'Just answer their questions, without amplification.'

'And have Isabel ready to scratch my eyes out for trying to involve them—'

'Don't worry,' Roger assured her. 'She'd never do anything so ill-bred.' He got up and stretched, and exchanged a glance with Antony in which he seemed to be trying to read the other man's thoughts. 'Jenny's tired if you aren't, Meg,' he said then, and held out his hand to her. 'Let's leave all this until tomorrow.'

## III

When the Maitlands had guests they usually borrowed Sir Nicholas's spare room on the first floor, but it had been too late for that so Jenny had made up the bed in the attic room, which was reasonably comfortable, and even reasonably tidy, but still definitely an attic. When she and Antony went to their own room she did not start to undress immediately, but seated herself in the easy chair that was pulled close to the electric fire. Antony removed his tie for the second time that night, and threw it down on the dressing-table. 'Do you still want to talk, love?' he asked. He sounded, not exactly resigned, but not enthusiastic either.

'I haven't done very much up to now,' Jenny pointed out, which was no more than the truth. 'Anyway ... just for a minute, Antony. Come and sit down.'

He crossed to the hearth slowly, and took the chair opposite her. 'Something's worrying you,' he said.

'I don't like mysteries.'

'I suppose you think I do.'

'No.' She did not comment upon the sharpness of his tone, but her eyes wavered away from him. 'There are two things I want to know.'

'If I can, I'll tell you.'

'I wonder.'

'Don't be enigmatic, Jenny. Of course I will.'

'In spite of what you said to Roger and Meg, you weren't keen on referring the local police to Inspector Sykes, were you?'

'Chief Inspector,' he corrected her automatically, considering his answer. 'It had to be done, and the result, I expect, will be just as I foretold it.'

'But—' said Jenny, and did not attempt to continue.

'I suppose you haven't forgotten that Sykes's immediate superior is Superintendent Briggs.'

'*Chief* Superintendent,' she said, mocking him. He met her eye then, and laughed reluctantly.

'*I do not love thee, Doctor Fell,*' he reminded her.

'Neither of you do,' said Jenny, not very lucidly. 'But the thing is, Antony, it doesn't matter, does it?'

'Not a bit, love. Except that if I meet him I shall most likely lose my temper, which is always a mortifying experience. And besides,' he added more cheerfully, 'if our paths do cross again can you imagine what Uncle Nick will say?'

Jenny shuddered, but she was obviously relieved by his change of mood. 'Don't worry, it may never happen,' she said consolingly. 'The other thing, Antony ... will you take me with you tomorrow night?'

His first reaction was a sharp denial. 'To meet Uncle Hubert? I most certainly will not!' She did not say anything to that, but went on looking at him hopefully. 'You wouldn't like him, love,' he went on, and now his tone was almost pleading.

'It isn't a matter of liking or disliking,' said Jenny. 'I want to know.'

'But he's such an old sinner.'

She smiled then. 'Do you think he'll contaminate me?' she said.

'Hardly.' He resisted the impulse to smile back at her. 'If I promise to tell you everything—'

'It isn't the same as seeing for myself what kind of a person he really is. And however good your intentions were, you'd be tempted to edit your material, you know.'

He would have liked to deny that, but found himself unable to do so. He said, weakly, 'But, Jenny, love—' and knew as the words trailed into silence that the argument was over already.

Jenny knew it too. She said, 'That's better!' in a satisfied tone, and then added, as the thought struck her that he might still be unconvinced, 'You can't say it's "just an

45

ordinary case", Antony. What touches Roger and Meg touches you, doesn't it? And, even if I weren't so fond of them both myself, what touches you touches me.'

'I'm sorry, love, I know how true that is.' He wondered, as he spoke, what he would have done if she had asked him to hold back from whatever of unpleasantness or danger might lie ahead; but that wasn't Jenny's way. He got up then and took the three paces that separated them, and bent to kiss her and rumple with his left hand the unnatural neatness of her curls. 'Let the future take care of itself, Jenny, and come to bed.'

## IV

Antony had to be in court in the morning, but Meg and Roger stayed with Jenny until about half past eleven, when the police intimated that they might have possession of their own home again. Fortunately Betty had not been sent away; she had been questioned, and then instructed to confine her activities to the kitchen. So she and Meg were able, in a couple of hours' brisk work, to remove the most obvious signs of alien occupation. Roger, who was a stockbroker, spent most of the time on the telephone. 'I'm sure you could conduct your affairs just as well from here as from the office,' said Meg, when she rejoined him.

The evening papers were already on the streets when the court adjourned for the day, and Maitland picked one up on his way back to chambers. He stood in the hall to study it for a moment, before going into his uncle's room, which looked, from the masses of documents that were strewed all around it, rather as though it had been struck by a cyclone. Sir Nicholas, however, seemed to have abandoned the study of his brief, and was reading a paragraph in his favourite journal under the headline, BELATED TRIUMPH OF THE JUS QUAESITUM TERTIO. Antony allowed him to finish, and lay the paper aside, before he spoke.

46

'There's something here that might interest you, Uncle Nick.'

Sir Nicholas took the proffered newspaper gingerly, as though he mistrusted this approach. 'I hope—' he began, but then his eye caught Meg's name and he broke off and read to the end of the paragraph in silence. The *Evening Chronicle* did not find too much that was sensational in the fact that Miss Margaret Hamilton's home had been broken into the evening before, while she was at the theatre, or even in the fact that a man had been killed, presumably in the sort of argument that occurs when thieves fall out. So far, they said, he had not been identified.

'Unpleasant,' said Sir Nicholas, when he had finished reading. He did not seem to think any further comment was necessary, but laid down the paper and sat waiting, his eyes on his nephew's face.

'The trouble is,' said Antony, not too much put out by this scrutiny, 'they've got it all wrong.'

'That was to be expected.'

'Yes, well, I'd better tell you.' He proceeded to do so, and was thankful that his uncle listened quietly. If he had been in one of his more captious moods the explanation might have taken twice as long, and even as it was it was complicated.

'I suppose you are going to tell me that you can think of half a dozen different reasons for this man's death,' Sir Nicholas said when he had finished. He sounded resigned, and Antony replied, with more emphasis than was strictly necessary,

'No, I can't think of one.'

'That, at least, is something to be thankful for. Your participation may then be confined to—er—to an advisory capacity,' said Sir Nicholas hopefully.

'Not if anything happens to involve Roger and Meg—to involve them any further,' Antony told him frankly. He thought it might be as well to get that clear from the start. But Sir Nicholas, who could never be absolutely relied upon to react as expected, gave an approving nod.

47

'You will, of course, be guided by events,' he agreed. 'Meg must not be worried, if that can be avoided, but once the police realise that what has happened is in some way a continuation of the events of seven years ago, there should be no danger of that.'

'That's what I *think*,' said Antony, relieved, and laid only the slightest stress on the word; he did not add that, like Meg, he had a feeling that things weren't going to be quite as simple as that. Perhaps there was no need to. Five minutes later they left for home together in perfect amity.

Roger took Meg to the theatre at the usual time, and called for the Maitlands with his car at about a quarter to eight. They had eaten early, and were waiting for him, but he had found a parking space in the square and was in no hurry to leave. 'I left Uncle Hubert with the port,' he said, stretching out in the chair that was understood to be his so long as Sir Nicholas wasn't present. 'He'll be quite happy till we get back.'

'How is he?' Jenny enquired, ready enough to settle down again and wait until Roger wanted to go. Roger laughed, with a nice blend of amusement and irritation.

'Incredible,' he said. 'Our last meeting might never have taken place. In fact, he's behaving exactly as if he'd just returned from one of the trips he used to take abroad. He was charming to Meg, most appreciative of all she had done for his comfort; and then had the cheek, when he got me alone, to reprove me for not providing her with a larger establishment and more servants. He supposed I was still squandering money which could be put to better use on the cottage at Grunning's Hole ... well, you know, Jenny, Meg loves it as much as I do.'

'Now that she's got it furnished to her taste,' said Jenny, but her tone was sympathetic.

'Yes, well, I must say it's more comfortable now,' Roger admitted. 'The yawl is an extravagance too, considering how little time Meg has to spare. I swear to you I felt sixteen again.'

'Prison life hasn't affected his health then?' Antony asked.

'He might have been away for a rest cure,' said Roger bitterly. 'He doesn't look a day older, and he hasn't even lost any weight, his suit fits him perfectly.'

'What about Meg, what's her reaction?'

Roger's voice softened, as it usually did when he spoke of his wife. 'Poor girl, she's bewildered. It would be easier, I think, if she'd ever seen him before, she'd know what an old humbug he can be. As it is I don't know—I honestly don't know how either of us is going to stand it.'

No use pointing out to him that the situation need never have arisen if he'd shown the least strength of mind. Antony could only be thankful that Sir Nicholas wasn't among those present. His comments would certainly have been scathing, whereas actually there was nothing for it now but to make the best of things. 'It needn't be for long,' he pointed out.

'No. Meg's going house hunting tomorrow, but you can see we had to ask him first what sort of place he wanted.'

'What was his answer to that?'

'Anything would do for him, a mere *pied à terre*. Mayfair perhaps, or Belgravia.' Jenny and Antony both began to laugh, and after a moment Roger joined them. 'It's not funny,' he protested. 'One way and another, it's been the hell of a day.'

'Yes, you'd better tell me about that,' said Antony, recovering himself. 'Jenny said you went home about half past eleven.'

'Well, I must admit the police had left everything in a fair old shambles. Finger-print powder over everything, and nothing in its place.' (Jenny had a private smile for that, because she had a theory that Roger himself never went into a room without disordering it completely within two minutes of his entry.) 'They'd washed the blood off the hall floor, which was a kind thought on somebody's part, but that left a clean patch, which shocked Meg, and she got one of her cleanliness is next to godliness fits, which carried

49

us over the next couple of hours. Then we got some lunch, and just as we were finishing the police arrived. Detective Inspector Rawdon and Detective Chief Inspector Sykes, with statements typed up for our signature, and the same questions to ask all over again.'

'Had Sykes put Rawdon into the picture?'

'Yes, I think so. At any rate, Rawdon seemed rather more friendly. As for Sykes ... you know he has a bland sort of way with him. He sent his respects to you both, by the way, since he expected I'd be seeing you.'

'That's all right then,' said Antony, referring rather to the first part of the statement than to the detective's message. 'Isn't it?' he insisted, when Roger seemed to hesitate.

'I can't say talking to policemen is my favourite way of spending an afternoon. And then, just as they were leaving, Uncle Hubert drove up in a taxi ... and even that didn't faze him.'

'What happened?'

'Sykes remembered him all right, I could tell that, but he didn't say so. Just waited for introductions to be made, acknowledged them politely, and took Inspector Rawdon away with him. And then I had to explain to Uncle Hubert what had happened, exactly as if the whole thing was my fault.'

'You have my sympathy.'

'I might believe that if you'd wipe the grin off your face,' Roger informed him sourly.

'Well, but ... look here. If you've got the police off your back that's the main thing, isn't it?'

'I don't know ... honestly, Antony, I don't know what to think.'

'What did Uncle Hubert have to say?'

'Just that he'd never seen or heard of the man since he went ashore from the *Susannah*.'

'Did you believe him?'

'As much as you ever can.'

'At least, he could tell you the man's name.'

50

'Sykes had already told me that ... William Stoker.'

'And he didn't take the opportunity to question Uncle Hubert ... no, of course, you'd have told me if he had.'

'I think perhaps if Meg hadn't been there ... I got the impression he liked her and didn't want to upset her more than was necessary.'

'That figures. In which case—'

'He may be back,' said Roger sadly. 'I'd thought of that already.'

'Never mind. Was that all Uncle Hubert could tell you?'

'I didn't press him. As you were coming tonight—'

'I see. Yes, perhaps that was the best thing. But that being so—'

'We'd better be getting along,' said Roger reluctantly. But he got up as he spoke.

'After all,' said Jenny, following suit with rather more alacrity, 'Uncle Hubert might like an early night.'


V

They found Hubert Denning comfortably ensconced in what Jenny and Antony knew perfectly well was Roger's favourite chair. There was an empty glass beside him, and he was now enjoying a cigar.

As far as Antony could see, Roger had been right, the old man hadn't changed in the slightest degree. He was of no more than medium height, and when he saw Jenny and came quietly to his feet it could be seen that his bearing was as erect as ever. For the rest, he had a round, pink face and fluffy, white hair, no scantier than it had been seven years ago; at the moment his blue eyes were benevolent but Antony—remembering how hard a stare they could assume at will—was no longer deceived into thinking that he had a childlike look.

Uncle Hubert came a couple of steps to meet them, took Jenny's hand into both his own, and murmured, 'Charming, charming,' in response to Roger's introduction. 'Sit

51

down, my dear,' he added, for all the world as if he were in his own home, and went on, as Jenny obeyed him, taking the chair opposite to his, 'Yes, Roger, I remember Mr Maitland perfectly well. The young man who is so fond of asking questions.'

'You may also remember,' said Roger disagreeably, 'that he has a habit of getting them answered.'

The old man ignored this. 'It was good of you,' he said, with something of pathos in his tone, 'to come out on a cold night like this to see me.' He went back to his chair again, and lowered himself into it with a sigh of satisfaction. 'This is very pleasant,' he said. 'Very pleasant indeed.'

Antony smiled, he couldn't help it, but Roger was blind, for the moment, to the humour of the situation. He said abruptly, 'I'll get you both a drink,' and went across to the cabinet in the corner of the room. Uncle Hubert exchanged a look with Jenny that quite openly deprecated whatever was *gauche* in his godson's behaviour. Antony seated himself at one end of the Regency sofa that had belonged to Roger's mother and said, with a note of apology in his tone, 'As to that, Mr Denning, I must admit that I had a motive for coming.'

'So Roger informed me,' said the old man, with gentle resignation.

'He has also told you, I suppose, what happened here last night.'

'He has, indeed.'

'The man who was killed was one of your former associates, as I understand it.'

'I should prefer to say an employee, Mr Maitland.'

'Perhaps that would be more accurate. Though there was a—a profit-sharing agreement, wasn't there?' said Antony solemnly.

Uncle Hubert shook his head in a minatory way, not at all deceived by this. 'It is not perhaps in the best of taste to make a man's death the subject of a joke,' he said. For some reason, Antony felt the short hairs rise at the nape of his neck, and was glad when Roger came across the room with a glass in each hand, relieving him of the necessity of replying immediately.

'Jenny,' said Roger, placing one of the glasses at her elbow. 'Antony. Will you have another glass of port, uncle?' He seemed to have got over his ill humour, and to be taking his tone from the other two men. Uncle Hubert, of course, had always been able to turn the most dire confrontation into something that sounded like a delightful social occasion.

'No, thank you, Roger, I have had quite sufficient.' There was something in his tone that made the simple offering and accepting of hospitality sound like the beginning of a debauch. Jenny, who had been about to take up her glass, let her hand fall into her lap again. Roger gave Antony a rather helpless look, shrugged his shoulders, and then went back to the tray for his own drink. 'Personally—' he said, as he rejoined them again. He did not, however, attempt to complete whatever thought had been in his mind, but sat down on a rather penitential chair that looked as if it had been designed for use as a *prie-dieu* rather than for sitting.

Antony said into the silence, 'This William Stoker—'

'I have already told Roger that I know nothing of his recent activities.' Mr Denning put down his cigar carefully in the ashtray beside him. 'How could I have heard anything, in my retirement?'

'From what my clients have told me from time to time, one is not completely cut off from the world.' The old man nodded his head, but did not comment on the statement. 'In any case,' Antony went on, 'he might have been in touch with you.'

'I can only assure you that he was not.'

'Never mind. Perhaps we can get at it another way.' He was already becoming as absorbed as he might have been by a witness in court. Jenny was sitting silent, and had recovered from Uncle Hubert's spell sufficiently to be sipping her gin and tonic; and Roger, too, had withdrawn himself from the orbit of their conversation, a thing which he did with surprising ease for so confident a personality. 'Where did he live?'

'In the main, on board the *Susannah*.'

'Was he married?'

'I believe not. As far as I remember—and my memory may well be at fault—he had parents living at Balham.'

'Do you remember their address?'

'I doubt if I ever knew it. In any case, after seven years—' He broke off, looking at Antony speculatively. 'What is your reason, Mr Maitland, for wanting this information?'

'We're all puzzled as to why this happened ... Stoker's death. Why in this house, the day before you were due here?'

'It may be merely a coincidence; he came here to steal, not having yet learned the error of his ways.'

'I don't like coincidences.'

'Nor I. But after all,' said Uncle Hubert indulgently, 'the man had to live.'

'Can't you think of any better reason?'

'Only the obvious one. You must have thought of that for yourself, Mr Maitland.'

'That he wanted to get in touch with you, and mistook the date of your ... arrival. Yes, of course. But that doesn't tell us why he was killed, or who killed him.'

'There, I'm afraid, I cannot help you.'

'What about his associates?'

'Now, that *is* an interesting question,' said Uncle Hubert, frowning over it. 'The members of my crew, you mean.'

'They'll do to be going on with.' He paused, and then added bluntly, 'Or are they all in prison?'

'Really, Mr Maitland!' said the old man, in mild protest. Obviously that was a remark that was lacking in taste, too. 'Two or three of them might be at liberty, but my memory fails me, I really cannot be sure.'

'Who knew you were coming out? Who knew you were coming here?'

'Roger and Meg. You and Mrs Maitland I suppose.'

'And the prison authorities.' Uncle Hubert inclined his

head. 'Nobody else?' Antony asked him, with more urgency in his tone.

'Not so far as I know.'

'I see. There's only one more question I can think of then: when Stoker lost his—his job on the *Susannah*, would he be in need of money?'

'In no immediate need, I daresay. In the long term ... that is something else I can't tell you, Mr Maitland.'

'Can't, Mr Denning?'

'Shall we say, I could hazard a guess? I cannot believe you would wish me to do that,' said Uncle Hubert with finality, and picked up his neglected cigar. 'This play of Meg's,' he went on, turning to Jenny and becoming benevolent again, 'have you seen it, my dear? Shall I enjoy it?'

Altogether they concluded, when the three of them were alone together on the way home, that round had been to him.


# VI

It wasn't yet time to collect Meg from the theatre, so Roger came upstairs with them and sank thankfully into one of the wing chairs by the fire, which Antony was occupied in coaxing into a glow. 'You see what I mean,' he said. 'What did you think of him, Jenny?'

'He gave me the creeps,' said Jenny. 'I don't think I'd have taken to him anyway,' she added doubtfully, 'if I'd met him before I knew what he was really like, I mean. But I'd never have guessed—' She broke off, shaking her head.

'A more important question,' said Antony, getting up from his knees, 'is, how far was he telling the truth?'

'Hardly at all, I daresay,' said Roger gloomily.

'Come now, I don't suppose it was as bad as that.'

'You think this man, this William Stoker, wanted to get in touch with him?'

'It seems likely. The thing is, why? And why on earth, Roger—this is something I *can't* understand—why on earth did Uncle Hubert want to stay with you?'

'Convenience,' said Roger. 'He's probably more comfortable than he would be at an hotel.'

'Yes, but if he's up to something—and Stoker's appearance in your house suggests that he may be—you're surely the last person he'd want around.'

'Whatever way you look at it, it doesn't make sense,' said Roger crossly. 'I suppose any minute you'll be telling me it's an interesting situation.'

'That's one way of describing it. It is also uncomfortable, and potentially dangerous.'

'Damned uncomfortable,' Roger agreed. 'Do you think someone may be gunning for Uncle Hubert?'

Antony, who had seated himself next to Jenny on the sofa, smiled at his hopeful tone. 'If we knew why William Stoker was killed—'

'We're just going round in circles,' said Jenny. 'You're trying to—what is it Uncle Nick says, Antony?—to theorise ahead of your data.'

'That's all very well,' said Roger, 'but what do you suggest we do?'

'I don't see what we can do until things become clearer.'

'That may never happen.'

'Well, wouldn't that be a good thing? Once you've found somewhere for Uncle Hubert to live you can forget all about it.'

'That's easier said than done, love,' Antony put in. 'I agree with both of you, as a matter of fact. We ought to do something, but I can't think what.'

'I'd agree with Jenny,' said Roger, 'I think I would, anyway, if it weren't for the possibility that someone we know stole Meg's latchkey.'

'Even if we knew that was true, it wouldn't help us much. But there is one thing I've wondered: who, besides your Sunday evening guests, knew Uncle Hubert was coming to stay with you?'

'Nobody really, except you and Jenny. Did you tell anybody, Jenny?'

'No, of course not.'

'Well, I told Uncle Nick, but I can't imagine him talking about it.'

'Betty knew, I suppose,' said Jenny.

'But she didn't know who he was,' Roger objected. 'The prison chaplain knew, for that matter.'

'And Stoker seems to have known, even if he'd got the date wrong,' said Antony. But he knew as he spoke that Jenny was right, there was nothing they could do but wait and see. After a little more argument, Roger agreed to this, and then it was time for him to leave for the theatre.

Neither Antony nor Jenny said much after he had gone. Jenny could see that her husband was worried, but she didn't think he was in the mood to answer questions. As for Antony, he felt that his forebodings were illogical, and better kept to himself.

Only one other thing happened that night, and that was after Jenny was asleep. The telephone rang and Antony got up and went into the living-room to answer it, but when he said 'Hallo', and repeated it sharply a moment later, there was no response at all. He couldn't hear the dialling tone, only, very softly, the sound of someone breathing.

After a while he became conscious that the room was growing cold, and that he hadn't waited to put on his dressing-gown. He replaced the receiver gently and went back to bed. A wrong number, a frequent enough occurrence; the only thing that was strange about it was that the caller had neither apologised nor rung off.

He slept badly that night, but by morning the incident had almost faded from his mind.

## Monday, 20th April

### I

The next day, which was Friday, Meg and Jenny went flat-hunting together, but without finding anything suitable. After that they didn't see each other until Sunday afternoon, when the Farrells came early to Kempenfeldt Square. They reported that Hubert Denning had only been out of the house once, to church that morning. He was as amiable as ever, which was getting on Meg's nerves. That was Roger's story. Meg, in the kitchen watching Jenny beat the eggs for a sponge cake, said only, 'It's having the *worst* effect on Roger, darling,' which might have been her sense of the dramatic running away with her, but on the whole Jenny thought not. Luckily, Sir Nicholas came upstairs then, as was his habit on Sundays, so the conversation reverted to neutral topics except for some routine questions from counsel on the subject of the murder, which Roger answered as briefly as he was able to without incurring a charge of evasiveness; as they lacked fuel for further argument, this was perhaps just as well.

On Monday morning, however, Roger phoned Antony to ask if he would be free for lunch; and Antony, abandoning without regret the idea of sandwiches at his desk and a quiet hour for the contemplation of the papers in a case of malicious wounding, agreed to meet him. It wasn't an absolutely unprecedented invitation, but in the circumstances he couldn't help wondering what had happened to prompt it.

Roger was waiting for him in the bar at Astroff's. He had commandeered a corner table, and the waiter had already been to take his order. He said, 'I've ordered two doubles,' and Antony nearly replied, 'Meg wouldn't approve of that,' but remembered in time that Roger knew nothing of their meeting five days ago. But perhaps it was because she was in his mind that he enquired instead,

'Does Meg know you're meeting me?'

'I can't see that it matters—'

'Just an idle question.'

'—but in any case the answer is, no.'

'I see.'

'I expect you do. I've something to tell you—' Their scotch arrived at that moment, and he waited until the waiter had left them again before going on, as though there had been no interruption, '—but the trouble is, you'll probably think I'm imagining things.'

'On the whole, I think that's unlikely.'

'We'll see.' Roger took a gulp of whisky, set the glass down firmly, and pushed it a little away from him as though eschewing temptation. 'I think I'm being followed,' he announced baldly.

'Do you though?' Antony was startled, but he knew Roger well enough to acquit him of sensationalism. 'How long has it been going on?'

'I'm not sure. I first noticed the chap—the daytime chap —on Friday, but it wasn't until the following day that I was certain what was happening.'

'Why didn't you tell me?'

'No sense in worrying Jenny, or Meg.'

'No. I see,' said Antony again.

'Do you believe me?'

'Of course.'

'Then I must say, you take it pretty calmly.'

Antony smiled at him. 'You're not exactly leaping about yourself. But I was wondering ... you said, "the daytime chap"?'

'It's a different one in the evenings.'

'Does he ... do they ... does either of them know he's been spotted?'

'I shouldn't think so.'

59

'You haven't tried to shake them off?'

'What would be the good?' He took up his glass again, and moved his other hand in a wide, dissatisfied gesture. 'My life is an open book,' he said.

'Yes, I daresay. But the thing is, Roger . . . why?'

'I haven't the faintest idea.'

'If it's some of Uncle Hubert's pals—'

'But why should they be watching me?'

'To make sure you're out of the house, perhaps, so that they can call on him undisturbed.'

'There wouldn't be any point in that during the day. Betty's there, if Meg isn't. No, what I was thinking, Antony, was . . . the police?'

'That opens up a whole new train of thought.' Antony tasted his scotch, found it comforting, and drank more deeply.

'They *look* like police,' said Roger, in the tone he might have used if the other man had been arguing with him. 'There's another thing too, they're younger than any of the *Susannah*'s crew would be.'

'In that case—'

'Perhaps they weren't satisfied with what I told them of my movements the night Stoker died.'

'Following you about now wouldn't help them to prove you went home that night,' said Antony positively. 'But if you really think . . . it would be as well, wouldn't it, for me to have a word with Sykes?'

'Do you suppose he'd tell you anything?'

'He might.'

'Then I wish you'd try. Because I don't mind telling you'—Roger picked up his empty glass and put it down again—'I find it a most unpleasant feeling, having some-body dogging my footsteps.'

'Don't worry.' (Easy to say, that.) 'There may be some quite simple explanation.'

'Such as what?'

'I'd have to give it some thought. But I'll tell you this much, Roger, I'd rather it was the police, however much you dislike the idea, than some undesirable characters from Uncle Hubert's past.'

'I suppose you're right,' said Roger. But he did not sound as if he found the thought particularly consoling.

## II

Maitland phoned Chief Inspector Sykes as soon as he got back to chambers, which was early, because Roger and Meg had to attend the inquest that afternoon. When he got through, his uneasiness was, if anything, doubled by the readiness with which the detective agreed to his suggestion of a meeting. A cafe in Victoria Street was named as a suitable trysting place, Antony having no desire to see the other man in the Inner Temple, and still less desire to visit him at New Scotland Yard. The malicious wounding papers were pushed aside, he called Willett in to tell him he was leaving, and went out without disturbing Sir Nicholas to say where he was going. His uncle's study of the duelling brief had not yet reached a critical stage, but even so his temper was uncertain.

Sykes was waiting for him. He didn't change much with the years, Antony reflected as he crossed the room to join him ... a square-built, fresh-faced man with a comfortable, country look about him and an unusually placid temper. 'Quite like old times, Mr Maitland,' he said by way of greeting. He had a pleasant voice, though nobody could have mistaken his north-country origin, and very often—as now—there seemed to be an undercurrent of amusement in it.

Antony said, 'I hope not!' rather abruptly, but then he smiled too. 'I hope too that I haven't dragged you away from something important,' he added.

'There was a conference,' Sykes told him. 'Well, I was glad of the excuse to get out of it. And then it fitted in with my own ideas, like. I'd been meaning to telephone you one of these days.'

'Had you though? What about?'

'It will wait, Mr Maitland. Let's have your side of it first.' He paused, looking around him. 'I ordered tea for both of us ... ah, here it is. Now we can talk without interruption.'

'I imagine you've got a very good idea what I want to say to you,' said Antony, accepting a cup of tea and ignoring the milk jug that was being pushed towards him.

'I expect it has to do with the murder last week in Beaton Street,' said Sykes. He added a fifth lump of sugar to his own cup, and gave his companion an encouraging look.

'It certainly has!' Antony spoke more forcefully than he had intended. 'I want to know, first of all, whether you people are having Roger Farrell shadowed.'

The Chief Inspector was stirring his tea and did not look up immediately. 'And if we are ... *if* we are, Mr Maitland ... what exactly has that got to do with you?'

'You know he's a friend of mine.'

'Yes, I see. I suppose you would consider that a sufficient reason for curiosity.'

'I would.'

'Then, as you're so well informed already, perhaps it will do no harm to tell you that your assumption is correct.'

'In heaven's name ... why?' He paused, and then added irritably, 'I seem to have been saying nothing else for the last few days.'

Sykes ignored this in favour of the question. 'I should have thought you'd know that without my telling you, Mr Maitland. This isn't the first time Mr Farrell has been mixed up in a murder.'

'But ... that's ridiculous! That other affair was all cleared up.'

'Was it? Nobody was arrested for Martin Grainger's murder,' Sykes reminded him.

'B-but—' said Antony again. He was beginning to lose his temper, and in contrast Sykes's placidity was very marked.

'The one thing we know for certain about Grainger is

that Mr Farrell's mother killed herself because he was black-mailing her,' the detective pointed out tranquilly.

'Yes, but ... l-look here, Chief Inspector, he t-tried his h-hand at b-blackmailing Hubert Denning too.'

'So you told us, Mr Maitland.' If the angry stammer in Antony's voice alerted him, he made no sign. 'Mr Denning wasn't tried for murder, if you remember.'

Antony looked at him helplessly. 'You withdrew the warrant for Roger's arrest,' he said, when the silence had protracted itself uncomfortably.

'That was because it was obvious, even before we talked to the DPP, that in view of the other things that had happened we couldn't hope to get a conviction.'

'Are you s-seriously t-telling me that you b-believe—?'

'I keep an open mind, Mr Maitland.'

'But B-briggs doesn't. Is that what you're t-telling me?' He stopped and made a desperate attempt to clutch at the rags of his temper. 'Is this his idea?'

Sykes smiled in his sedate way. 'The Chief Superintendent is in charge of the investigation,' he said, not committing himself.

'But, even if you suspect Roger, what can you hope to gain—?'

'No new evidence about the murder, I agree with you there. You'd know, however, I daresay, that not all the gold from the bullion robberies was recovered.'

'I thought ... no, I remember quite well, Chief Inspector, one lot was recovered from the *Susannah*—'

'That's quite correct.'

'And one of the crew—one of the gang, I suppose I should say—gave away where the rest was hidden abroad, in the hope of getting a lighter sentence, I suppose.'

'You'd learn that from the newspaper story, I daresay. Very misleading the newspapers can be sometimes,' said Sykes reflectively. 'What perhaps they didn't print was the rather important fact that gold bar to an approximate value of £1,000,000 was unaccounted for. It is believed,

63

(a) that it never left the country, and (b) that it constituted Mr Denning's private hoard.'

'How do you make that out?'

'Because that's the only way we can account for the ignorance of the man who helped us, literally, with our enquiries.'

'That's reasonable, I suppose. But how does all this connect with Roger?' Antony demanded.

'Mr Denning is an old man. If he wishes to recover the gold he will need some assistance.'

'Have you tried asking him where it is?'

'He has been asked many times, but refused so much as to admit its existence.'

'That does sound as though ... but he'd never ask Roger for help. They're not on those sort of terms. Have you forgotten what happened on board the *Susannah*?'

'I don't think I've forgotten anything, Mr Maitland. There seemed to have been some sort of a falling-out between them, certainly, but that does not preclude the possibility that previously they had been on friendly terms.'

'You're tying R-roger in with the b-bullion robberies, then, as w-well as with the m-murder?'

'Try looking at the thing from our point of view, Mr Maitland. Mr Denning is staying in the Farrells' house ... but, as I said, I have an open mind.'

'I believe you.' He sounded merely tired now, not angry any longer. 'Will you give me some information, Chief Inspector ... without prejudice?'

'If I can,' said Sykes cautiously. 'But perhaps before we go on I'd better tell you what I wanted to talk to you about.'

'As you please,' said Antony, rather listlessly.

'First, because you may be wrong about Roger Farrell—'

'I'm not.'

'—and if you are there is always the possibility—the probability—that at some point you might find yourself in trouble with the law.'

'I thought by now you knew me better than that.'

'Let's say it's very easy to let loyalty outrun discretion.'

'Come now, Chief Inspector, you've commended my discretion before now.'

'I'll grant you know how to hold your tongue. But I never commended your common sense,' said Sykes bluntly. He paused to let that sink in, and then went on, 'If, on the other hand, your friend is innocent of anything more serious than stupidity in harbouring Hubert Denning—'

'I could never explain that to you,' said Antony, depressed.

'*If* he is innocent,' repeated Sykes impassively, 'you might both be in danger of a different sort. If Stoker's death was a gang killing, as seems likely—'

'Wait a bit! What do you know about him?'

'Up to six years ago, nothing. Until Mr Farrell told us, we had no idea he had anything to do with the bullion robberies, but it is a fact that only since the rest of the gang went to prison has he been running with Boney Nelson's mob.'

Antony closed his eyes for a moment. His sense of humour seemed to be reasserting itself. 'I can't *wait* to tell Uncle Nick,' he murmured. And then, more strongly, 'Who the hell is Boney Nelson?'

'Now, I thought 'appen you'd have heard of him,' said Sykes, maddeningly vague. 'Has none of your clients ever mentioned him to you?'

'If I knew who he was, I wouldn't be asking you,' Antony pointed out.

'Then I suppose I'd better tell you. He's one of the most troublesome, and *so far* the most invulnerable, villains around in London at the present time,' said Sykes. Antony thought the detective was probably unconscious of the emphasis, but it wasn't in his nature to allow it to pass unremarked.

'That sounds as if you thought his immunity might not last for ever,' he said tentatively. Sykes gave him an indulgent smile.

'That's as may be. But you can believe me when I tell

you that he's mean, and he's brutal, and not without cunning; and his word is law to about thirty or forty other choice specimens ... including the late Bill Stoker.'

'I see. What's his line?'

'Protection ... drugs. Anything that turns up that has money in it, particularly if it's dirty.'

'You don't seem to like the gentleman, Chief Inspector.'

'I don't,' said Sykes, more emphatically than was usual with him.

'Even so, I don't quite see your argument. I'm not to concern myself with Stoker's death, I suppose that's what you mean. But why should Boney Nelson object if I do so? From what you tell me, Stoker was a henchman of his.'

'To quote the newspapers,' said Sykes, shrugging, ' "when thieves fall out—" '

'You're afraid I might stumble on a trail that led to Nelson. On the other hand, if I leave you to it, you'll waste time trying to prove that Roger—'

'You ought to know by now, Mr Maitland, that I only want the truth.'

'I know.' He did not sound as if the idea cheered him much. 'I'll even grant that it's what Briggs wants, consciously at any rate; but that doesn't prevent him from being an obstinate, pig-headed old bastard. And, as you told me just now, he's in charge of the investigation.'

The detective sighed. 'I can see I'm not persuading you,' he said. 'Will you believe me in this, at least ... Boney Nelson is dangerous.'

Antony did not reply to that directly. Instead he asked, 'What do you think happened, Chief Inspector?' and sounded genuinely curious.

'I haven't enough facts at my disposal on which to base a theory,' said Sykes, selecting his words with care. 'On the face of it, it seems most likely that Stoker went to the Farrells' house to meet Mr Farrell, and that he had been given a key so that he could wait indoors, instead of hanging about in the street. Someone—not necessarily Mr Farrell—followed him there and killed him.'

'I suppose I should be grateful even for the benefit of so much doubt,' said Antony, too thoughtful for the moment to lose his temper again. 'But if that were true Roger would have found the body during the evening, when he went home alone to meet Stoker.'

'Can you be sure that he didn't?'

'Yes, absolutely. Apart from anything else, he'd never have let Meg run blind into a situation like that.'

'You may be right, Mr Maitland.' Sykes's tone was altogether too balanced, too open-minded for Antony's taste. 'It's no use our quarrelling,' the Chief Inspector continued mildly, when he saw that his companion was about to speak. 'I seem to remember you had some questions you wanted to ask me.'

'I thought perhaps—'

'I can't promise to answer them until I know what they are,' said Sykes patiently.

'All right!' But he paused a moment to collect his thoughts. 'I gather Nelson has never been inside,' he said then. 'What about Stoker?'

'He's been lucky too.'

'Maddening for you,' said Antony, too politely. 'What about his former associates, the members of the crew of the *Susannah*? Are any of them out of prison yet?' Sykes pursed his lips, as though considering whether to reply, and he added in a rallying tone, 'Don't tell me that hasn't been looked into, Chief Inspector.'

The detective acknowledged this with one of his equable smiles. 'I can't see the harm in telling you,' he said. 'Two of them came out about a year ago, and are also believed to be with Boney Nelson now.'

'Leading correct and upright lives?'

'So far as we can prove.'

'Was one of them by any chance the chap who told you where the gold was hidden abroad?'

'He was.'

'I see. Will your kindness extend far enough to allow you to tell me their names and addresses?'

'I'm afraid not, Mr Maitland. I don't want your death on my conscience,' said Sykes precisely.

'I'd promise not to haunt you.' He waited a moment, but the detective made no effort to speak again. Antony gulped some of his lukewarm tea and pushed the cup across the table to be replenished. 'You must think me a fool,' he said.

'Let's just say, you're not the most cautious person in the world,' said Sykes carefully.

Antony laughed. 'Uncle Hubert says Stoker's parents are alive, living in Balham. Does the ban extend to them too?'

'You can find their address in the phone book, so I may as well tell you. They live at number 13, Mayridge Road, not far from the station. To save you the trouble of seeing them though, I may as well tell you, too, that Bill Stoker was living at home for "about six years", which tends to confirm what Mr Farrell told us.'

'Did it need confirmation?'

'It is always gratifying,' said Sykes primly. 'But about the old people: they profess not to know what "work" their son did, just that he seemed to have sufficient money for his needs. A respectable couple, he was a builder's foreman ... retired now. Stoker never brought friends home, or spoke of any of his acquaintances.'

'Too good to be true,' said Antony glumly. 'They must know more of him than that.'

'They're his parents, they probably took good care not to know anything more. As for what they suspected, you can hardly expect them to malign him now.'

'I suppose not. Do I thank you for that bit of information, Chief Inspector?'

'I admit I can't see that it will do you the slightest good,' said Sykes blandly. 'What are your other questions?'

'They concern the actual murder. What, for instance, was the time of death?'

'The doctors put it at about eight o'clock, give or take a little either way.'

'I see.' As expert witnesses, they wouldn't be swearing

68

very definitely to that in court, the opportunities for effective cross-examination were too good. Still, for the moment, and as far as the police were concerned, it put Roger's alibi definitely on the scrap heap. 'How did he die?' he asked.

'He was stabbed.'

'Yes, I saw that for myself.'

'A flick-knife,' said Sykes. Antony laughed again, and sounded for the moment genuinely amused.

'This is as bad as drawing teeth,' he said. 'My own impression was that the blow had been struck upwards ... an expert job.'

'You may be right,' agreed Sykes placidly.

'I'm sure I am. I was badly brought up, Chief Inspector, but I can't imagine that Roger's naval training qualifies him as an expert in the gentle art of murder. A normal man's instinct would be to hold the knife so'—he demonstrated with his left hand—'and strike downward.' The detective said nothing, but his look of amusement deepened, and suddenly Antony was annoyed again. 'Oh, all right, behave like a s-sphinx if you want to. What about the key?'

'What about it?'

'Forget this nonsense about Roger handing one over to Stoker.'

'The maid, Betty, seems reliable enough.'

'That leaves the one that Meg lost.'

'I reckon nowt to that, Mr Maitland. Stoker had no chance to get hold of it, nor had any of his associates.'

'Somebody who had an opportunity might have handed it over, just as you say Roger did.'

'If you will forgive my saying so, Mr Maitland, the Chief Superintendent found that story of Mrs Farrell's a little too circumstantial.'

Antony said, 'B-briggs!' as though it were an imprecation. And then, 'I suppose he thought *I'd* invented it.'

'He has always,' said Sykes, 'had a great respect for your ingenuity.'

'You'll be telling me next that *you* b-believe it.'

'Nay, I wouldn't go as far as that.'

'Have you even b-bothered to go to s-see any of those six people?'

'I must admit—'

'No, of course you haven't! Well, I'll do that bit of your job for you,' said Antony savagely, 'and if your Boney Nelson takes umbrage, at least that will be informative.'

Sykes eyed him consideringly for a while, but did not again remind him of the possible danger. Instead he sighed and said, 'If I knew what you're trying to prove—'

'Nothing! Anything! Like you, I want the truth.' His anger, never very durable, had faded now. 'And if you're going to remind me that I'm less open-minded than you are, I can only say ... I know Roger, you don't.'

'Then we may as well leave it there. Would you like some more tea, Mr Maitland?' But Antony was already on his feet. He said goodbye briskly, and left the detective dribbling the last few drops of tea into his own cup. He walked back to chambers, fast enough to over-heat himself even on that grey and chilly day; and completely failed to concentrate for the rest of the afternoon on the papers on his desk, which old Mr Mallory had been kind enough to re-arrange during his absence.

### III

He debated as he walked home, this time at a more reasonable pace, on whether he should make some excuse to be alone with Roger while he reported on his conversation with Chief Inspector Sykes, or whether it would be better to tell Jenny now exactly what was the police point of view. That also included, of course, mentioning Boney Nelson, and he still hadn't reached a decision when he got to Kempenfeldt Square. When he let himself into number 5, Gibbs was hovering at the back of the hall.

Gibbs was a disagreeable old man, of deceptively saintly appearance, who ought to have retired years ago from his post as Sir Nicholas's butler if it hadn't been for the fact that he enjoyed being a martyr. He came forward now, when he saw Antony, and said as though it was an accusation, 'There was a person on the telephone, asking for Mrs Maitland.'

A 'person' might mean almost anybody, from the Archbishop of Canterbury down. 'Did you give him our number?' Antony asked, not very interested.

'He already knew it, he said, but could get no reply. Unfortunately, I did not see Mrs Maitland when she came in.'

'Was there a message?'

'He did not even leave his name,' said Gibbs, making it sound as if that was an additional source of grievance, and all Antony's fault.

'Never mind, I'll tell her,' said Maitland, and went on up the stairs. But Jenny didn't seem much interested either. She had a *distrait* air, which wasn't like her, and it wasn't until they were both on their second glass of sherry that she suddenly said, 'That man, the one Gibbs told you about ... it must be the same one.'

'The same one as what?' asked Antony idly.

'He called me again, about ten minutes after I got home.'

'Well?' Jenny didn't answer immediately and he turned to look at her. 'Who was it? What did he want?'

'He didn't tell me his name.' She picked up her glass and sat looking into it as though she were crystal-gazing. Antony was aware of a stab of alarm. 'As for what he wanted, he said he wanted to speak to me particularly. He said he'd tried before, only you answered the phone.'

'I don't ... yes, I do remember. Last Thursday or Friday night, after you were asleep.'

'Why didn't you tell me?'

'He didn't say anything, just breathed at me. I thought it was a wrong number.' He paused, and then added more urgently, 'What did he want to say to you ... particularly?'

'It was a message for you. I don't know why he had to give it in this roundabout way.' She closed her eyes for an instant, groping for the exact words, and then opened them

71

again and said, looking at him directly now, 'He said, "Tell your husband if he's wise he won't interfere in Hubert Denning's affairs." And then he laughed, as though he'd said something funny, and that was all.'

'He rang off?'

'Yes, while I was still asking him what he meant.'

'What did he sound like?'

'Horrible!'

'Yes, love. I meant—'

'Rather a deep, growly voice. Cockney, but only just.'

'I see.'

'Who was it, Antony?'

'I don't know, love. But fair's fair, and I'd better tell you what's been happening today. It started with Roger joining me for lunch ...'

Boiled down to essentials, it wasn't a long story. Jenny was frowning thoughtfully by the time he had finished. 'Do you think this—this Boney Nelson is after Uncle Hubert's gold?'

'It seems likely, especially in view of what you've just told me.'

'But you've no interest in that.'

'He doesn't know it. He's probably arguing on the same lines as the police, that Roger and Uncle Hubert are conspiring together. And as I'm known to be a friend of Roger's—'

'Antony, I don't like it at all.'

'Neither do I, love.'

'Because if the police suspect Roger you've more or less got to concern yourself, haven't you?'

'That's how I see it. Don't worry, Jenny. If we can find out who took the key that may be enough to get the police off Roger's back. It may be just a family matter, no gangsters involved in it at all.'

'In that case,' said Jenny unanswerably, 'who rang me up today?' He had to admit she had a point.

They still hadn't dropped the subject for more than a few minutes at a time when Roger arrived after dinner.

So then the story was to tell over again, once Roger had been asked about the inquest and had reported its adjournment with no evidence taken except that of the doctors, and of identity, of course. 'Uncle Hubert's keeping damned quiet about it, if that's what he's up to,' said Roger, when Antony had finished an account of his talk with Sykes.

'But don't you think the fact he refused to tell the police where it is means he wants it for himself?' asked Jenny.

'Not necessarily,' said Roger, and Antony added by way of further explanation, 'If I were in prison I wouldn't feel inclined to help the chaps who put me there.'

'All the same—'

'All the same, love, the police think he's after it; and so does some gang or other, on the evidence of the phone call and also of the murder ... which is evidence in its way, even though we don't understand it. And both sides think Roger is associated with Uncle Hubert.'

'It seems,' said Roger reflectively, 'as though our only course is to lie low and say nothing.'

'I don't agree with you there. I did explain to you, didn't I, that the police think you're the most likely person to have handed over a key to William Stoker?'

'Yes, but—'

'Sykes admitted they weren't following up the question of the one Meg lost. They don't believe in it.'

'It's so unfair,' Jenny protested, but both Antony and Roger, more or less simultaneously, said in a rather depressed way,

'I can see their point.'

'Well, I can't!' said Jenny. 'But I agree with Antony, Roger, it would be a good idea to find out who took the key.'

'Can you?'

'I can try,' said Antony. 'Leaving the theatre on one side for the moment, because it seems on the whole unlikely that the key was abstracted there, the people who had opportunity at your house on Sunday night are Sam Reade, Leonard Watson, and this Victor Barham you mentioned.'

'Or Irene, or Isabel, or even young Terry,' said Roger.

'Yes, I must see them all.'

'I don't see how that will help,' Jenny objected. 'If any of them took the key they'll deny it.'

'So they will, love. But somebody may have seen something significant. Do any of them know any gangsters, Roger?'

'Boney Nelson?'

'Probably, in view of Stoker's connection with him.'

'It sounds unlikely in the extreme.'

'Any of the men might know him ... as a client, perhaps.'

'Well ... perhaps. What are you thinking, Antony?'

'That if we could prove a connection—'

'I don't honestly think—'

'Don't be so charitable. It's the only line open to us at the moment.'

'I suppose it is. But I really meant, do you think one of them coveted Uncle Hubert's gold and got in touch with a gangster to help him look for it. How would he know it existed, in the first place?'

'He wouldn't. It must have been the other way around ... Boney Nelson heard about the gold from one of Uncle Hubert's former crew members, and got in touch with somebody he thought would be able to help him acquire a key to your house.'

'But why should he want one?'

'That's another question, and I don't know the answer. I shall be in court for the rest of the week, at least I think so, so I'll have to see them in the evenings. Do you think any of them will actually throw me out?'

'It all depends,' said Roger seriously.

'Never mind. Who lives may learn.' He got up, suddenly purposeful. 'For heaven's sake, let's have a drink, and forget all about it for five minutes at least.'

But Uncle Hubert's affairs were still very much on his mind when he saw Roger out, two hours and several drinks later. He hesitated a moment in the hall, wondering whether he ought to talk to Sir Nicholas that night. But then he saw that there was no light in the study and the door was standing ajar, and didn't know whether to be glad or sorry that the decision had been taken from him.

## Tuesday, 21st April

### I

He phoned Roger's partner, Sam Reade, next morning, and got his rather grudging agreement to be at home, with Mrs Reade, in the late afternoon. Maitland was in court for the rest of the day, but when the adjournment came he left Willett to go back to chambers with his books and papers, satisfied himself that he had enough money in his wallet, and hailed the nearest cab. The Reades lived at Twickenham, and if it hadn't been Tuesday he would have got Jenny to drive him there; but on Tuesday, from time immemorial, Sir Nicholas came to dinner, a fugitive from the cold collation with which it had once been his house-keeper's habit to regale him on her day out. Jenny, there-fore, had her hands full, and in any case it wouldn't do for them both to be out when Uncle Nick arrived.

The house was exactly as he remembered it, large and rambling, and the drive was just as badly in need of repair. He thought he heard the cabbie swearing under his breath as they turned between the gateposts and bumped their way to the front door, and remembered Jenny saying that even if you were rich you probably had to choose your luxuries. Spending money on his surroundings didn't seem to be on Sam Reade's list. He asked the cabbie to wait, and went up the steps and used the knocker; he had some vague recollection that the doorbell didn't work. There was the sound of scuffling inside, and then the door was flung open by a girl who looked to be about fifteen. She had a round face and dark hair that fell to her shoulders without any concession to style, and when she saw him she said, 'Oh!' obviously both surprised and disappointed. And then, 'I'm sorry, I thought you were someone else.'

Some sort of an apology for failing to meet her specification seemed to be in order. 'I'm sorry, too,' he said, and smiled at her. 'It's your father I want to see.'

'He isn't back from the office yet.' She pulled the door a little wider as she spoke and he could see, as well as the remembered background of golf clubs and tennis racquets which apparently had been put down at random around the hall, another, slightly smaller girl, who could only be her sister, and who seemed to have got a fit of the giggles. 'Mummy's in. Would she do?'

'Admirably well.' The smaller girl giggled again at that, and her sister turned to frown reprovingly at her before stepping back and saying, 'Come in.' But her notions of formality ended there. She smiled at him graciously, it is true, but gestured at the same time towards the room at the left of the hall. 'In there.'

Antony said, 'Thank you,' and went towards the door, which was standing ajar. As he approached it, it was opened wider by a fair young man whose face looked vaguely familiar.

'Mr Maitland,' he said, and held out his hand. 'You don't remember me, of course. David Reade.'

'Of course,' said Antony, disagreeing with him, because now he felt he should have known who he was straight away. David must be in his middle twenties now, and he had grown his hair into a long bob, though it was clean and looked well brushed. Otherwise he had changed very little, being something over middle height and slimly built, and with a still rather boyish cast of countenance. Inexplicably, he seemed to be regarding Maitland with decidedly more pleasure than normal politeness would command.

'Come in,' he invited heartily. 'Irene's here, and I don't suppose Dad will be long.'

'Did he tell you—?' said Antony, following him into the room.

'Oh, yes, we knew you were coming. Anyway, I was expecting you to turn up. Ever since I knew what Roger had done.'

This too seemed inexplicable, but Antony was given no time to enquire into it. They had reached the circle of chairs that surrounded the fire, and David drew back to leave him a clear view of Irene Reade.

And here memory had been at fault. He recalled clearly enough that she was Sam Reade's second wife and David's stepmother, and he remembered thinking when he met her briefly seven years ago that she looked too young for the job, but he was quite unprepared to find her strikingly beautiful, with hair that was almost black, dark, lustrous eyes, and features that were classical in their regularity. Her greeting wasn't quite as enthusiastic as David's had been, but still her smile was warm and welcoming, and Antony, who was already well aware of the difficulties ahead, began to feel decidedly uncomfortable. Sam Reade, when he arrived, would greet him gruffly; he expected that and could deal with it. This unquestioning friendliness was something else again.

So presently he found himself sitting opposite her, in a large, shabby, comfortable chair, with David hovering beside him offering sherry or a martini. 'Mrs Maitland was with you when you came here before,' Irene was saying. 'How is she?'

'Very fit, thank you. Yes, sherry will be splendid,' said Antony, still not at his ease. And added, when David brought a glass and set it on the table at his elbow, 'Why did you say you were expecting me? And what has Roger done?'

'Why, taken in the old boy ... Hubert Denning,' said David, as though this should have been obvious. 'I knew as soon as Dad told me that there'd be trouble about that.'

'And where there's trouble—' said Antony lightly, and smiled at Irene, who looked as if she didn't quite like the way the conversation was going.

She leaned forward now and said seriously, 'We know you're a good friend of Roger's, Mr Maitland. It's only natural—'

'Yes, perhaps.'

David said buoyantly, 'There's been a murder, and you can't deny you've sometimes been able to help the police.'

'That's an equivocal phrase, don't you think?' He meant to say that lightly too, but he didn't like the reminder of the publicity that had sometimes attended his activities, and that hadn't always been favourable, and in spite of himself his voice was stiff.

'I didn't mean it that way,' said David quickly. 'I might just as well have said that you've helped innocent people.'

'You will see, Mr Maitland,' said a deeper voice from the doorway, 'that we are giving Roger the benefit of the doubt.' Sam Reade came into the room and pulled the door shut behind him. Antony, not without difficulty, managed to extricate himself from the embrace of his armchair.

He thought his host's remark was better ignored and said only, inanely, 'It was good of you to see me,' and thought as he spoke that if he couldn't find anything better to say he might as well keep quiet.

'As to that—' said Reade, and left the sentence unfinished. He came across the room and bent to kiss his wife, then chose the chair next to hers and leaned back in it, relaxing deliberately. 'Sherry, David,' he said, without looking round.

Antony sat down again, and let his eyes follow David as he went across the room to the table that held the drinks. Then he looked back at Reade again. 'I gather I needn't explain my errand to you.'

'We've met before, Mr Maitland.'

'Yes.'

'And again Roger finds himself in difficulties, and again you are trying to involve me in his affairs.'

'That isn't exactly true.'

'I'm sure,' said Irene, 'that if you would let Mr Maitland explain—' Her husband held up a hand as though in protest, and she let the sentence trail into silence. David came back with a glass in his hand and set it down clumsily, spilling some of the sherry. He said, before his father could

79

speak, 'Roger's your friend,' and it sounded like an accusation.

'My partner,' Reade corrected him. He was a square-built man, not quite as tall as his son, with alert grey eyes, a fierce moustache, and a good deal less hair than he had had seven years ago. Then he had been wearing rather shabby tweeds and there had been an air of relaxation about him; but today, dressed for the City, he looked altogether more formidable. Also he seemed to be in a mood for plain speaking, though his tone was one of almost excessive amiability. He smiled at Antony, and added pleasantly, 'He doesn't choose to ask my advice in managing his private affairs.'

'You knew, however, that Hubert Denning was going to stay with him.'

'He told me as much, after it was all arranged.'

'That's one of the things I wanted to ask you, Mr Reade. Did you mention the fact to anyone else?'

Irene said, 'There, you see!' and laid a hand on her husband's sleeve. Obviously she found the question reassuring. David chose this moment to sit down again, but as he looked from Maitland to Reade he was frowning slightly.

'It wasn't,' said Sam dryly, 'the kind of information I should be likely to broadcast, either to friends or business acquaintances.'

'No, I see that. But you did bring up the subject on Sunday evening, when you were visiting in Beaton Street.'

'Did Roger say that?'

'Isn't it true?'

'I expect it is. I can't be sure.' He glanced at his wife. 'Do you remember, my dear?'

'I think it was you who brought the subject up, Sam.'

'Oh, well then, I expect I thought the others already knew about it.'

'I see. And you, Mrs Reade. Did you tell anybody?'

'No. I'm quite sure of that. Except—this is something you must have forgotten, Sam—we both mentioned it in front of David.'

80

Antony turned his head. 'What about it, David?' he asked.

'I didn't *tell* anybody. Terry and I talked about it, though ... Terry Barham,' he added when Maitland's look became enquiring. 'But, of course, she knew about it anyway.'

'Could anyone have overheard your conversation?'

'They could, I suppose. We were having dinner at that Danish place in Duke Street. But it doesn't seem very likely that anyone was near who was interested in what we were talking about.'

Antony thought it was very unlikely indeed, but he only said vaguely, 'We have to cover all the angles,' and turned back to Reade again. 'How well do you know Hubert Denning?' he asked.

'Slightly. He was a close friend of Roger's parents, you remember. I knew him through them.'

'I was wondering if you had any knowledge of his friends, or business associates. Anybody he might have confided in.'

'What sort of a confidence would you have in mind?'

'Perhaps nothing more incriminating than the date he was coming out of prison, and where he was going to stay. If you can think of anybody he'd be likely to ask for help in recovering a quantity of gold he's got salted away somewhere, that would be even better.'

'*Gold?*' said David, before either his father or stepmother could speak. It was certainly a question, but perhaps even more an expression of disbelief. Irene gave a gasp that was almost equally revealing.

'According to the police not all the missing bullion was accounted for,' said Antony, as though apologising for putting forward an opinion not his own.

'And you think—' That was Reade. He too sounded incredulous, and broke off apparently in despair of finishing his sentence in a coherent way. David took up the question where his father had left it.

'Do you think there's some connection between the murder, and the gold, and Mr Denning coming out of prison?'

'Well, after all, the dead man, Stoker, must have had some reason for being in the Farrells' house.'

'You think Denning may have been in touch with him?' Reade asked.

'I don't really think anything at all ... yet.' He paused, and looked from Sam, to Irene, to David, who had bounced to his feet again, as though too excited to sit still. 'I was asking you, Mr Reade, if you knew of anybody—'

'Well, I don't,' said Sam Reade shortly. 'And it's no use putting the question to Irene, because she knows even less of Denning than I do.'

'So I understand. I'm sorry if my questions offend you. I thought that, in view of your—er—relationship with Roger—'

'If he dislikes the situation that has arisen, he has only himself to blame.'

'You said you were giving him the benefit of the doubt.'

'What has that got to do with it?'

'Everything, I should have thought.'

'I was being ironical. Nobody has seriously suggested—have they?—that Roger murdered the man.'

'The possibility seems to have occurred to the police.'

'Has it, indeed?' Reade sounded shocked.

David said impulsively, 'I told you what would happen, Dad.'

'So you did.' Uncharacteristically, Reade's lips were compressed to a thin line. 'In that case I must ask you, Mr Maitland, can you do anything to help him?'

'I'm doing my best.' Antony was apologetic again.

'You must forgive me if I don't quite see why you came here.'

'I had hoped my questions were self-explanatory.'

'Not to me.'

'That's a pity, because there's one more question I wanted to ask you.'

Reade's expression showed no sign of softening. 'Please listen to him, Sam,' said Irene, and again laid her hand for a moment upon his arm.

Her husband did not look at her, but said, 'I suppose I must,' ungraciously.

'It concerns the evening you and Mrs Reade spent with Roger and Meg last Sunday.'

'What about it?'

'Did you happen to see Meg's handbag—a large, rather flat, black one—lying on the chest on the upstairs landing?'

'It may have been there, I didn't notice,' said Sam grudgingly.

Irene took the time to smile at him before she said, 'I saw it there, of course. It was a very beautiful one.' It was an indulgent smile, Antony thought, very much what she might have given to a fractious child. He turned to her with relief.

'At some time during the evening it was moved from the landing to the bathroom. Do you happen to know when that was?'

'No, I—I should have noticed that, Mr Maitland.' For some reason it occurred to him at this point, for the first time, that the pearls that gleamed softly against the flattering background of her black dress were unquestionably genuine. 'I mean,' Irene went on, explaining herself rather earnestly, 'I might not have noticed it was gone from the chest, but I couldn't have missed seeing it in the bathroom, unless it was put away in the airing cupboard with the towels.'

'It was left on the window ledge.'

'In that case—' she began, but Sam interrupted her, saying violently,

'What the hell is all this?'

'I was hoping you wouldn't ask me that.'

'I *have* asked you,' Reade pointed out.

'Meg lost her latchkey.'

'I suppose you think one of us took it.'

'And I was trying so hard to avoid giving you that impression,' said Antony ruefully. He wasn't quite sure why, but Reade's complaint struck him as funny, and he had to make a conscious effort to keep the amusement out of his voice.

'In any case, I don't understand your interest,' said Sam huffily.

'Stoker, and his murderer, had to get into the house somehow,' said Antony patiently. He didn't like the necessity for explanations, but had to admit that Reade had a right to ask for them. 'The police incline to the view that Roger is the most likely person to have opened the door, so naturally, I am concerned to show that somebody else might have done so.'

'One of the people who were at dinner that night?'

'That is only one possibility, though in view of the fact that the handbag was moved it seems a likely one. If you will look at it from Roger's point of view for a moment, I think you will agree that I have to explore it.'

'We both understand that, Mr Maitland,' said Irene quickly. Sam gave a sort of growl that might have been agreement, but was far more likely dissent.

'It means asking you to try to remember your own movements that evening, and also those of the rest of the party. If the handbag wasn't in the bathroom on the last occasion you were there, Mrs Reade, we need only consider what happened after that time.'

David gave a sudden crack of laughter. 'If you're going to ask Mrs Wilson how many times she went upstairs during the evening I wish I could be there,' he said. Antony, who well remembered the streak of prudishness that was so unexpected in Roger's sister, smiled sympathetically, but did not attempt to reply. It was only a matter of time before Sam Reade erupted again, and he wanted Irene to have the chance to answer him before that occurred.

She was obviously giving the matter her serious attention. 'I went upstairs after dinner, while Meg was making the coffee and everybody else was in the drawing-room,' she said. 'When we left I had to fetch my coat, of course, but I didn't go into the bathroom then.'

'How long did you stay after dinner?'

'A little over an hour, I should think.'

'We came away at about half past ten,' Reade put in, and David added *sotto voce*,

'With a consciousness of duty well done.' His father gave him a black look, but did not attempt any more open comment, but Irene said in a worried tone,

'I'm afraid that's how Roger and Meg look at it ... that we have to exchange hospitality every so often, because of Sam being Roger's partner, you know.'

That was too near the truth for comfort, and anyway the conversation was straying sadly from the lines he had laid down for it. 'Who else went upstairs during that after-dinner period?' Maitland asked.

'I don't really remember. It's all very well for you to laugh, David,' Irene added good humouredly, 'it just isn't the kind of thing one notices.'

'Not if one is nicely brought up,' said David, with an unnaturally solemn look. 'But I'll tell you what, Mr Maitland, Terry might remember.'

'Miss Barham? I shall ask her, of course.'

'What I should like to know,' said Reade, coming forcefully back into the conversation and speaking in a hectoring tone, 'is whether you are assuming that whoever took the key also killed Stoker?'

'I don't think that would be a fair assumption on what we know at present.'

'No, but he'd be an accessary, wouldn't he? Before the fact,' said David, with satisfaction.

'That depends,' said Antony cautiously. He was aware of David's goodwill, and amused by it, but he couldn't help wishing that, for the moment at least, he wouldn't be quite so outspoken.

'Well, I remember, if Irene doesn't,' said Reade unexpectedly. 'All the women were up and downstairs at one time or another during the evening. I went out into the hall myself to fetch some cigars, and Leonard Wilson came downstairs while I was there. I don't think Victor was out of the room at all, but I might be wrong about that. Does that satisfy you?'

'I'm grateful,' said Antony, and drank some of the sherry that had been standing neglected beside him.

David watched him for a moment and then said, 'But is that *all*?' He sounded ludicrously disappointed.

'All I can think of.'

'When are you going to see Terry?'

'Tomorrow or Thursday, at about this time. That is, if she and her father are willing to see me.'

'Make it Thursday and I'll be there,' David offered eagerly.

'The trouble is, I can't decide whether you'd be a help or a hindrance,' said Antony frankly. He finished his sherry and got to his feet.

This time, David didn't seem to be at all cast down by this plain speaking. He grinned and said, 'I'll see you out,' and moved ahead of the visitor towards the door.

So Maitland made his farewells, and was surprised when Irene Reade held out her hand to him, so that he had to cross the hearth-rug to take it. 'We're always pleased to see you,' she said, 'and if there's anything at all we can do to help—'

'I expect Roger will let you know,' said Antony. He glanced at Reade, who evidently hadn't missed the dryness of his tone, for his expression had become sardonic.

If Irene had noticed it too she wasn't going to say so. Instead, 'It must all be very upsetting for Meg,' she said. In face of which understatement there didn't seem to be anything else to say, so he smiled from one of them to the other and followed David out into the hall.

David didn't speak until they were outside the house and the front door was closed behind them. Then he said regretfully, 'You don't want to take any notice of Dad. He's mad as fire to think of Irene being mixed up in anything so sordid.'

'I shouldn't call visiting the house several days before the crime being mixed up in anything,' Antony told him.

'You're here, aren't you?' said David, as if this left no room for argument. 'I say, do you really think Mr Wilson is mixed up with this man, Stoker?'

'For heaven's sake, don't go around saying things like that,' Antony implored him.

'Well, it stands to reason, if somebody took Meg's key it must have been him,' said David. Antony would have liked to explore the logic of this, but decided on second thoughts that the subject was, perhaps, better left alone. 'I wish I'd been there, but Terry will be able to help you,' David went on. 'Will you go and see her on Thursday?'

'That's up to her, and her father.'

'Oh, Terry won't mind.'

'That's good,' said Antony, without any great faith that his companion was speaking the truth. But David continued without taking any notice at all of his rather hollow tone.

'What do you think is going to happen next?'

'I wish I knew.' He thought about that for a moment. 'Or perhaps I don't,' he added. 'Perhaps I'm happier not knowing.'

'You're taking it for granted that the murder must have something to do with Mr Denning going to stay with Roger and Meg. That means ... do you think the dead man was part of a gang?' David asked hopefully.

'What I think is that I've done enough talking for one day,' said Antony, and set off down the steps towards the waiting taxi. He didn't turn again until he had the door open and his retreat secured, but then he said, 'Goodbye, David. I'll see you on Thursday, with luck,' and got in and shut the door firmly against any further questions.

II

Gibbs was in the hall and gave him a sour look as he went in. Upstairs there was a savoury smell, a warm room, and Jenny and Sir Nicholas drinking sherry in the firelight. A tranquil scene. He paused in the doorway, because he had never ceased to savour the moment of homecoming and Jenny's welcoming smile, but when he started to cross the room it was immediately apparent that the tranquillity was only surface deep. His uncle moved to the attack without bothering to return his greeting.

'Jenny tells me you're meddling again.'

'I didn't say anything of the kind,' said Jenny, without heat. Antony smiled at her.

'I know, love. You were only explaining. Anyway, Uncle Nick, I don't know what you're complaining about. You said yourself that Meg mustn't be worried.'

'I never dreamed,' said Sir Nicholas, steam-rollering over this counter-attack without difficulty, 'that you were proposing to get mixed up with the police.'

'You can hardly call talking to Sykes—'

'I don't know how else you would describe it.'

'The thing is, Uncle Nick ... look here, I'd better explain it to you properly.' Jenny grimaced at him, but she was used to having her own attempts at explanation criticised, and bore no malice. 'I'd have told you about it last night, only you'd gone to bed by the time Roger left; and there hasn't been a chance today.' He went over to the desk where the tray was standing, refilled his uncle's glass and Jenny's, and poured sherry for himself. On the whole, the wine was more likely to have a mollifying effect on Sir Nicholas's mood than any amount of words.

'I shall be glad, of course, to listen to what you have to say,' said Sir Nicholas austerely.

Antony brought him up to date as briefly as possible, neglecting only to mention the anonymous telephone call that Jenny had received, but the story wasn't told without interruptions and his temper was wearing thin as he came to the end. 'So I thought I'd better see the people who had the best chance of taking the key,' he concluded.

'Do you really think—?'

'It may not be a likely explanation, but it's a better one than that Roger let Stoker in himself.'

'So far I agree with you. But it cannot be said to exhaust the possibilities.'

'Don't you think the fact that Meg's handbag had been moved—?'

'Cannot Meg herself help you as to when that occurred?'

'She says not.'

'I can't understand why she didn't notice until next morning that it had been taken into the bathroom,' said Sir Nicholas petulantly.

'That's because you weren't at Beaton Street while they were doing the alterations. There's a second bathroom that can only be reached through Meg and Roger's room; and that, of course, is the one they use.'

'I see.' Sir Nicholas pondered for a moment, and in the silence Jenny started to say something and then thought better of the idea. 'What you have told me of the police reaction makes me uneasy, very uneasy,' said Sir Nicholas at last. 'If Superintendent Briggs is in charge of the case—'

'There's nothing to be done about that, Uncle Nick.'

'Nothing at all. Unless you could be persuaded to conduct yourself sensibly, which I suppose is too much to hope for,' said Sir Nicholas gently.

'I haven't done anything so far, sensible or otherwise, except go to see the Reades this evening.'

'That, I agree, could not perhaps have been avoided. But you have advised the police of your interest in the affair, which in the circumstances cannot be said to be an advantage, either to yourself or to Roger.'

'They'd have assumed my interest in any case ... don't you think?'

Sir Nicholas compressed his lips, and did not reply to that directly. 'May I remind you that you have not so far given me any account of your talk with Mr and Mrs Reade.'

'It wasn't particularly helpful.'

'Even so—'

'The handbag hadn't been moved when Mrs Reade went upstairs after dinner, or so she says. Sam Reade maintains that both the other women and Leonard Wilson were upstairs at some time after that; he himself went into the hall at one point, but he doesn't admit to having gone any farther.'

'Are they telling the truth?'

'Your guess is as good as mine.'

'You're quite right, my dear boy, I wasn't inviting you to advance an opinion for which you have no grounds,' said Sir Nicholas in a honeyed tone. Antony caught Jenny's eye and grinned at her. 'Are you telling me that your visit was a complete waste of time?' his uncle went on, coldly observant of this by-play.

'When I've seen all the people who were present that evening it may be possible to—to conjecture who is telling lies,' said Antony meekly. Sir Nicholas gave him a hard look.

'If any of them are,' he remarked, and picked up his glass, as though dissociating himself from the whole distasteful business.

'Yes, of course,' Antony agreed. 'There's a further complication, however, that I haven't mentioned yet. Do you remember David Reade, Jenny?'

'I met him when I drove you to Twickenham that time,' said Jenny, with only a moment's hesitation. 'He'd just got a new sports car, and looked at ours as if it was some sort of an antique.'

'That's right. He was there too. No, I don't mean at Beaton Street ... just now when I was talking to Sam and Irene.'

'Is the fact relevant?'

'It may be. I've only told you what they said, haven't I, not their reactions? Sam was gruff, I don't think he's ever really liked Roger, or feels particularly ready to put himself out to help him; Irene was conciliatory; David was all eager interest—I imagine, incidentally, that he's on better terms with Irene than he is with his father—but he could have been putting it on.'

'This must be leading somewhere,' said Sir Nicholas hopefully.

'Only to another conjecture, I'm afraid. He's obviously on good terms with Terry Barham. She could have taken the key and given it to him.'

'And how do you propose to tie him in with this—what was the name you gave me?—this Boney Nelson?' enquired Sir Nicholas fastidiously. And then, without waiting for a reply, 'I might have known it was only a matter of time before you entangled yourself in the affairs of—er—of a gang.'

'It isn't the first time,' said Jenny incautiously, rather as though this might serve to reconcile Sir Nicholas to a state of affairs he obviously deplored. 'Before Uncle Hubert went to prison—'

'You don't need to remind me. The whole business was botched and mismanaged to an incredible degree.'

It seemed as well to ignore this. 'None of my suspects —if you will allow me so positive a word, Uncle Nick—is tied in overtly with the criminal element involved. But if Boney Nelson foresaw a need for the key and approached one of Roger's friends with a view to getting his hands on it, he might have preferred to talk to a young man, who might even see something romantic in the search for hidden gold.'

'Anything might be expected of a youth who takes— what did you call it?—an eager interest in your affairs,' said Sir Nicholas repressively.

'Well, I do think it's a possibility we should bear in mind.'

'You are proposing to talk to Roger's sister and her husband, and to—what was the name?—Barham and his daughter,' said Sir Nicholas; but now his tone was reflective. 'I can see you are in a fair way to becoming universally beloved.'

Antony grinned at that. But he'd had enough of the subject for one evening, his uncle could no longer complain of being kept in the dark, and he sought in his mind for some source of distraction. 'How are you getting along with that brief, Uncle Nick? The one about the duel?' It was no doubt a dangerous topic, but probably not as dangerous as a continued discussion of Roger's affairs.

'I cannot conceive,' said Sir Nicholas bitterly, 'what possessed Mallory to accept the papers.'

'I should have thought it presented some ... well, some interesting points.'

'What do you know of the history of duelling?' enquired Sir Nicholas. It was obvious from his tone that he expected a reply.

'Nothing much,' said Antony cautiously. But after a moment's thought he added, 'Now you mention it, can't you appeal to history, though? Surely the practice is an extension of the old trial by battle?'

'Did you know that law was on the statute book until 1818?' asked Sir Nicholas, suddenly amiable again, and interested in his subject. 'But it has been repealed now, and in any case would hardly apply.'

'No, I suppose not. But there must be some precedents.'

'Oh, there are. In the reign of George III, apparently, one hundred and seventy-two duels were fought, ninety-one of which resulted in fatalities. Only two of the survivors were executed.'

'Well then!'

'On the other hand, they *were* executed. One, a Major Campbell, as late as 1808. There is no doubt about the view taken by the law. As far back as Coke—'

'You said your chap was challenged.'

'But can it be said, in today's climate of opinion, that he was bound to accept? He went out with a gun in cold blood,' said Sir Nicholas, making the worst of a bad job, 'and deliberately shot his opponent.'

'You're both so busy with the legal aspects,' Jenny complained, 'that you're missing out the really interesting point. Why were they fighting?'

'The answer to that is a trifle complicated.'

'They must have had some reason.'

'Yes, of course. The real reason, I take it, was that "my

chap", as your husband so elegantly phrases it, was the lover of the challenger's wife.'

'That's better,' said Jenny, pleased that some human interest had got into the conversation.

Sir Nicholas became austere again. 'I am glad you think so,' he said.

'Well, go on, Uncle Nick. You said the *real* reason.'

'It is not the custom in affairs of honour to compromise a woman's name,' said Sir Nicholas, as though that should have explained everything.

'So what did they do?' asked Jenny impatiently.

'The ostensible cause of the dispute was that the challenger took exception to the tie my client was wearing,' Sir Nicholas told her, and looked pained when both his listeners began to laugh.

After that it was dinner time, and because Sir Nicholas never encouraged idle speculation the talk turned to other topics than Uncle Hubert and the dead man in Beaton Street. But Antony wasn't surprised when the phone rang at about ten o'clock, and again when he answered it nobody spoke. He said only, 'Wrong number,' as he came back to the fire, but he was pretty sure his uncle hadn't missed the sudden flare of anxiety in Jenny's eyes.

## Wednesday, 22nd April

### I

He had decided to drop in on Leonard and Isabel Wilson without warning, because he was pretty sure that if he telephoned in advance there would be some excuse why it wasn't convenient to see him that evening. So again he took a taxi as soon as he came out of court, and arrived at the small, too perfect house a little before five o'clock. This time it was a foreign girl who came to the door, Spanish, he thought, but she spoke English well enough, so he never had the opportunity to find out. She left him in the hall while she went through a door on the left; there was a murmur of voices from the room beyond, and then she came back with Leonard Wilson hard on her heels.

'Mr Maitland, how nice!' he said. He had a light, pleasant voice, with a curious quality of tone that made his most innocent remarks sound faintly sarcastic. Now he added, taking Antony's hand and shaking it warmly, 'You will forgive me if I say that I regard you rather as a bird of ill omen.'

'I wouldn't say you're altogether wrong about that,' said Antony. Wilson rubbed him up the wrong way, and always had, but there was no denying he was easier to deal with than his wife. He was a slender little man, very neat in his appearance, with dark hair worn fashionably long and a carefully trimmed imperial.

'I knew it,' he said now, triumphantly, and led the way back into the room from which he had come. 'My dear,' he said, 'here's Mr Maitland. I gather from his rather carefully chosen remarks that Roger's in trouble again.'

The room was long and narrow, its furnishings a little

too near perfection for Antony's taste, but even so there was no denying that Isabel Wilson dominated her surroundings. She was a tall woman, fantastically like her brother and just as sturdily built. Handsome, in her own way. She did not trouble to make the visitor feel welcome, but said, 'I might have known!' in tragic tones. It occurred to Antony that after seven years he had solved the problem of whom she reminded him ... one of Bertie Wooster's aunts, the unfriendly one. But all would be lost if he allowed her to take the initiative.

'I'm hoping you'll answer a few questions for me,' he said.

'What has happened now?'

'Gently, my dear, gently! Hadn't we better sit down,' Leonard suggested.

Antony said, 'Thank you,' rather doubtfully. None of the chairs looked as if it had ever been sat in before. He chose, after a moment's hesitation, one upholstered in a golden-brown brocade, as being the least likely to be contaminated by his presence.

'That's better,' said Leonard, sitting down too. 'Now, what is amiss? Is it Uncle Hubert, or is it the burglar?'

'I hold no brief for Roger,' said Isabel unnecessarily, 'and in the case of Uncle Hubert I consider he has behaved abominably. But I suppose no one can blame him because that unfortunate man was killed in his house.'

'I wonder,' said Wilson, his eyes on Antony's face.

'In a way, it is to do with both those things,' said Antony, with an apologetic look at Isabel because he was ignoring her interjection. 'The dead man wasn't a burglar, as the papers said; he was a former—a former associate of Uncle Hubert's.'

'One who got out of prison before him,' suggested Leonard brightly.

'One who escaped the round-up and never went to prison at all,' Antony told him. He thought sadly that he was making heavy weather of his explanations. 'It seems there must be some connection—'

'That may be true, but how can *we* help you?' said Isabel angrily.

'When did you first hear of Roger's action ... that he had asked Hubert Denning to stay with him?'

'I don't see—'

'If you will be patient, my dear, I am sure Mr Maitland's motive will appear,' said Leonard in his deceptively gentle way. 'We first heard on a Sunday evening—a week ago last Sunday—when Meg had asked us to dinner.'

'I don't think Roger had the slightest intention of telling us,' Isabel complained, 'if Mr Reade hadn't mentioned the fact.'

'Still, after that you knew Uncle Hubert was coming out of prison. Did you also know which day?'

'I believe Thursday was mentioned.'

'I see. Do you mind telling me, did either of you acquaint anybody else with those facts?'

'Good heavens, no!' said Isabel, as though the suggestion itself affronted her.

Leonard only smiled and said, 'No,' and did not attempt to elaborate on his reply. Isabel rounded on him and said furiously,

'Is that all you have to say? As far as I can see Mr Maitland is implying that one of us—one of *us*—might have been in contact with some low criminal.'

'But we agreed—didn't we, my dear?—that his coming here at all presaged some unpleasantness,' said Wilson blandly.

'That doesn't excuse—'

'I wasn't actually insinuating anything of the kind,' said Antony, looking from one of them to the other. He thought of adding, 'If the cap fits—' but it was no part of his plan to anger them without good reason. 'As you didn't tell anybody, perhaps you may have some ideas on the question of whom Mr Denning himself may have told.'

'Couldn't you ask him that yourself?'

'He says no one knew except the prison authorities. I'm not sure whether that is true.'

'Come now, that's better!' said Wilson, the sarcasm in his tone very marked now. 'We might almost imagine that you were asking us questions because you expected us to tell the truth.'

'A lie might be equally revealing,' said Antony composedly.

'Oh, do you think so?' Wilson thought about that for a moment. 'Do you know,' he said, 'I don't think I agree with you.'

'How you can sit there, Leonard,' said Isabel, almost speechless with indignation, 'while I—while we are being insulted—'

Her husband looked interested. 'What do you suggest I do?' he enquired.

'Refuse to answer! Tell him to leave!'

'I might do either or both of those things,' said Leonard reflectively, 'if I weren't still curious ... what has all this to do with you, Mr Maitland?'

'I'm acting on Roger's behalf—'

'Unofficially?'

'Not in a professional capacity,' Antony agreed. 'In view of your relationship I think he has a right to whatever help you can give him.'

'Last time you were here you threatened us with a scandal,' said Wilson, still thoughtful.

'So I did. But I was sure there was no need to remind you of that.'

Leonard laughed, and when he spoke he sounded, for the moment, genuinely friendly. 'But where, in this case, does the scandal come in? My dear wife, of course, would prefer that the murder had taken place anywhere else in the world, but the one account that appeared in the press mentioned Meg's stage name only, not Roger's.'

'The police,' said Antony, 'seem to be working on the theory that (a) Roger and Mr Denning are acting together to recover a quantity of gold bullion that was unaccounted for at the time of the trial; and (b) that Roger let the dead man into the house himself, or provided the key for someone else to do so ... with the obvious corollary that he is, if not the principal, at least an accessary to the murder.'

There was no doubt about it at all, he had the attention of both of them now, and perhaps Isabel's comment should not have been unexpected. 'It's all his own fault,' she said. 'I told him how it would be.'

'You foresaw the murder?'

'No, of course I didn't,' she snapped. 'But something was bound to happen if he persisted in such a flagrant disregard of the conventions.'

The impulse to say something that would further shock Isabel's intolerant self-respect almost overcame Antony's caution. It cost him something of an effort to say quietly, 'I could think of another way of putting it. The question is, however, are you going to help him?'

'I suppose we must.'

'Then have you any idea whom Mr Denning might have communicated with when he was due to come out of prison?'

'He certainly didn't get in touch with *us*,' said Isabel quickly.

'I never thought—' But now that he did think of it, who would be a more likely confidante than the 'niece' of whom he was so fond, and who had always seemed to be fond of him? 'It just seemed more likely that you'd know his friends than that Roger would.'

'Well, of course. But after what happened I can't think of anybody—'

'Sam Reade, for instance.'

'They were barely acquainted.'

'Mr Barham, then.'

'They were friends, certainly, but Victor wouldn't have anything to do with Uncle Hubert after—after he was arrested.'

'Can you be sure of that?'

'Oh, I think so.'

'At least,' said Leonard, smiling, 'he professed to be as shocked as we were at what Roger proposed.'

'I see.' They might be answering in good faith, and they

98

might not, there was no telling. 'There remains the question of the latchkey,' said Antony, not very optimistically. 'The house wasn't broken into, so somebody had one ... Stoker, or his murderer.'

'I can't see how we could be supposed to help you about that,' said Isabel disagreeably.

'Has Roger an alibi?' her husband asked.

'I'm afraid not. However—'

'Let us by all means assume his innocence,' said Wilson enthusiastically. 'Anything else would be too inconvenient.'

'I was going to say, he is quite sure nobody could have borrowed his key to have a duplicate cut.'

'In that case, surely their servant—'

'It's a possibility, of course. But it rather pales to insignificance beside the fact that Meg actually lost her key.'

'But who, finding it, would know—?'

'I should have said, she thought she lost it. It seems most likely that it was taken from her handbag during the evening you spent at the Farrells' house, a week ago last Sunday.'

'Mr Maitland!' said Isabel, outraged.

Leonard had an amused look. 'Now why should you think that, I wonder?'

'Because Meg's handbag was moved from the chest on the landing, where she always leaves it, into the bathroom the visitors used. Someone might have taken it in there to search at leisure. Besides, no one else had been to the house between Saturday afternoon, when she let herself in with it, and Monday morning, when she found that it was missing.'

'Meg is such a scatterbrain,' said Isabel scornfully.

'Do you think so? I'd have said she had her fair share of common sense myself.'

Wilson waved a hand airily, dismissing the argument. 'The point you're making is that one of the visitors that evening must have taken the key.'

'It seems the most likely explanation.'

'Oh, no. You will forgive me for saying that I think the police theory much more likely.'

'That Roger ... I don't believe it.'

'I can see you don't. And, of course, I can assure you that both Isabel and I earnestly hope you're right. Still, I trust you're not wedded to the idea that one of us took the key. It would make things so awkward, wouldn't it?'

'I've an open mind,' said Antony. (That was what Sykes had said, wasn't it? And for all I know it may have been true in his case.)

'What exactly is it that you want to know?'

'If either of you noticed what time the handbag was moved into the bathroom. Who was upstairs during the evening, particularly before that time?'

'That's rather a lot to ask of one's memory, isn't it? I was certainly upstairs myself during the evening, but I didn't notice anything out of the way. For that matter, I don't remember seeing the handbag at all.'

'Do you remember who went upstairs after you did?'

'Sam Reade was in the hall when I came down; he had his overcoat in his hand, so I suppose he wanted something from the pocket. I don't know whether he came straight back into the drawing-room or went up to the bathroom first. I seem to think that all the women were up and down at some time or other, and that possibly Victor Barham stayed put. But who went before whom I haven't the faintest idea.'

'That's what I was afraid of,' said Antony gloomily.

But Leonard now seemed inclined to be helpful. He turned to his wife. 'What about you, my dear?'

Isabel had a heightened colour. 'I have no recollection at all,' she said stiffly.

'Well, at least, when you went upstairs to fetch your coats ... was the handbag still on the chest then?'

'I didn't notice.'

'Did either Terry or Irene go into the bathroom at that time?'

'I did *not* notice.'

Wilson turned to Antony and spread his hands, as though disclaiming responsibility for his wife's unhelpfulness. 'I'm afraid we can't help you,' he said.

'Never mind.' He hadn't expected anything else from Isabel, but Leonard was unpredictable and there had been just a chance ... Antony came slowly to his feet. 'I'm grateful, at least, that you gave me so much of your time,' he said, and added, not altogether sincerely, 'Goodbye, Mrs Wilson. I'm sorry if my questions upset you.'

Isabel inclined her head in rather a stately way. Leonard had got up too, with perhaps more alacrity than was really polite. 'I'll see you out,' he said.

'Are you still with Bramley's Bank?' Antony asked idly, making conversation, as they came out into the hall.

'Now what in the world, I wonder, is the significance of that question?' said Leonard, coming to a full stop, so that Antony had to stop too and turn to face him.

'No significance,' he said, as lightly as he could. But suddenly he was interested in the answer. Leonard seemed to sense his change of mood.

'You're wondering—aren't you?—what would be my reply if I were offered a share in Uncle Hubert's gold,' he said. His eyes were opened wide with an innocent look that Antony well remembered, but there was malice in his tone.

'I might have asked you that question if I'd thought there was any chance of getting a straight answer,' said Antony equably. Wilson laughed aloud.

'Now you're being honest with me,' he said. 'Shall I reciprocate? You never know, I might be tempted if I knew how much was involved.'

'I see.'

'As to my job, I'm still with the bank but I moved to Head Office from Fenchurch Street about three years ago. That doesn't leave you much wiser, does it?'

'Not much.'

Leonard stepped past the visitor to pull the front door open. 'Incidentally,' he said, 'you mustn't mind Isabel. She

101

has a very delicate mind. And I do hope you'll try and restrain Roger from making a scandal. Neither of us has any influence over him at all.'

'I'll do my best,' said Antony dryly, and went out into the cool evening air. But he was very thoughtful as he crossed Walton Street and made his way towards the Brompton Road, where he had a reasonable chance of finding a taxi. He had never been in any danger of underrating Leonard Wilson, and now, perhaps, less than ever.

## II

Roger came round for a report that evening, and was amused by Antony's account of his enquiries, especially of Isabel's reaction to them.

'It seems to me you have no proper family feeling,' said Jenny severely. But she relented enough to be diverted in her turn by the latest news of Uncle Hubert, who had turned down with contumely all the flats that she and Meg had so far been able to offer him.

'It isn't funny,' said Roger sadly. 'I'm beginning to think we'll never be rid of him.'

There was no telephone call that night.

*Thursday, 23rd April*

## I

Unexpectedly, Antony was back in chambers not much after eleven o'clock the next morning, the case with which he was concerned having come to an abrupt halt owing to the illness of the defendant, who had been removed to the prison hospital with acute appendicitis. So he was at his desk when Hill phoned through with his usual air of apology to say that Mrs Maitland and Miss Hamilton would like a word with him if he was free. As it was already twenty past twelve he wasn't in much doubt that what they really wanted was lunch, so he went out to join them without more ado.

The bar at Astroff's was crowded, but they got a table that an earlier arrival had just vacated. 'Now,' said Antony, when the waiter had taken their order, 'what's this in aid of?'

'You can't grudge us a meal, darling,' said Meg, falling automatically into the role of ill-used womanhood, 'when we've been working our fingers to the bone.'

'I don't believe a word of it.'

'Well, wearing out shoe-leather, anyway.'

'That's more like it. I don't exactly grudge you lunch,' he added carefully, 'but I can't help wondering—'

'We've found a marvellous flat for Uncle Hubert,' said Jenny buoyantly.

'No better than the one overlooking the park that we found for him on Monday. He won't take it,' Meg prophesied ... Cassandra in person.

'He can't say this one is too small.'

'Then it'll be too big, or he won't like the outlook, or

'... to tell you the truth, darlings,' said Meg, looking from one of them to the other, 'I don't think he has the faintest intention of leaving us just yet.'

'You're making him too comfortable, Meg.'

'It isn't anything I do. He has a—a natural aptitude for making the best of a situation.'

'Is he still keeping to the house?' Antony asked.

'No. He goes for a quiet walk each morning, down to Cheyne Walk and a little way along the Embankment. But that's beside the point, darling. I don't think it's doing any good to Roger's image with the police, his staying with us.'

Antony gave a startled glance in Jenny's direction, but she was looking at Meg and did not meet his eye. 'What makes you say that?' he ventured.

'You needn't play the innocent,' said Meg, without rancour. 'There's been a man following Roger about, I couldn't help noticing when he fetches me from the theatre. So last night I asked him and he told me what Inspector Sykes had said. And I must say, darling, I don't think it was quite the thing for you to keep that to yourself.'

'I didn't, I—'

'Without telling me.'

'Well but ... look here, Meg, you're not always completely frank with Roger yourself.'

'There should be perfect confidence between husband and wife—'

'That's just what I'm saying.'

'—but not necessarily between wife and husband,' Meg concluded. 'That's different.'

'Well, all I can say is—'

'I know, darling. You're the soul of discretion and I don't know what either of us would do without you,' said Meg, cooing unashamedly. Perhaps it was as well that the waiter returned at that moment. Antony, as so often in her company, was torn between exasperation and amusement. When the man had gone he took a good pull at his drink before he said with decision,

'*I* can't do anything about Uncle Hubert.'

'If you mean that Roger should, I don't think it's reasonable of you,' Meg objected. 'He says he doesn't want even Uncle Hubert's murder on his conscience.'

'It might not come to that.'

'Darling, it was you who suggested it to him. Wasn't it?' said Meg. 'He also says for all he knows Uncle Hubert may really be a reformed character—'

'I don't believe that for a moment,' said Jenny. And when they both looked at her, surprised by this very un-Jennylike remark, she added with less assurance, 'If he *had* reformed he'd tell the police where the gold is.'

'That's exactly what I told Roger,' said Meg. 'But it's no use discussing it, because all he said was "Not necessarily", and went into one of his worrying silences.'

'Did he tell you,' asked Antony, 'about my talk with the Reades, and with Isabel and Leonard?'

'Oh, yes, he told me *that*. And it didn't really help much, did it? I've been thinking,' said Meg, in a rather forlorn tone that was completely foreign to her, 'suppose everything just goes on, as it is now, for ever.'

'It can't,' said Jenny. 'Things never do.'

'Well, I suppose in time even Roger would see that we can't keep Uncle Hubert indefinitely. And the police would stop following him about, but they'd still suspect him; and for all we know other people might too.'

Antony had a nasty feeling that things weren't going to solve themselves so easily, but there was no use pointing that out so he remarked instead, bracingly, 'I don't suppose you dragged me from my work just to tell me that.'

Meg immediately became animated again. 'You don't think we'd waste your time, darling. Either of us.'

'I wouldn't put it past you.' Meg and Jenny exchanged a glance. 'I know ... "you pity my ignorance and despise me",' said Antony, exasperation momentarily coming to the fore. 'But I'm damned if I'm going to play guessing games about what you want.'

'You may as well tell him,' said Jenny.

'Well, of course, that's what I'm here for,' said Meg, in tones of sweet reason. 'Only it isn't very nice, darling. You see, I had a phone call this morning, just before I left to meet Jenny.'

'I'm beginning to see,' said Antony, but not as though the prospect gave him any pleasure.

'So I told Meg about the man who rang me,' said Jenny. 'And, Antony, he said almost exactly the same thing. "Tell your husband not to interfere in Hubert Denning's affairs if he values his own safety."'

Antony looked from one of them to the other. They were both alarmed, both doing a pretty good job of hiding it; it showed in Jenny's animation, a little too exaggerated to be real, in Meg's airiness. 'If I remember rightly, the threat this time is slightly more explicit,' he said after a moment. 'What about the man's voice, Meg?'

'London, but educated. Half educated, anyway. And I'll tell you something, Antony ... he was enjoying himself.'

'Have you told Roger?'

'I will tonight, of course. It didn't seem the sort of thing to phone him about at the office, and I know he had a luncheon engagement. Besides, I thought you might be able to tell us what to do.'

'I don't suppose this chap, whoever he is, is referring to your flat-hunting activities, Meg.'

'You mean, we aren't doing anything, so just go on that way.'

'That's right.'

'Well, I wondered. You've seen Isabel and Leonard and the Reades already, there's nothing to be done about that. But ought you to call off your visit to the Barhams?'

'Why?'

'In case it comes under the heading of interference.'

'I hardly think—'

'You don't know,' said Meg stubbornly. Jenny said nothing at all, but he could feel her unspoken anxiety as if it were his own, and his reply was directed to her as much as to Meg.

'Let's analyse the situation. It seems fair to assume that Uncle Hubert would like to collect the gold from wherever he hid it, but his movements are watched and he's playing it cannily. Unfortunately, someone else is after the gold too ... most likely Boney Nelson, briefed by the two men Uncle Hubert likes to consider his former employees. They think, wrongly, that Roger and I are on Uncle Hubert's side, but until we make some overt move to confirm that suspicion I don't see that there's any danger.'

'What I'd like to know,' said Jenny, 'is why they phoned *us*.'

'Playing on your womanly fears, love.'

'Well, as far as I'm concerned that was good psychology,' said Meg candidly. 'I'm scared stiff.'

'I told you—'

'That's all very well, darling. Unless I'm mistaken you think there's some sort of a tie-up between Boney Nelson and one, at least, of the people who came to our house the night my key went missing.'

'It seems a fair assumption.' Antony sounded cautious.

'Then action against that one would be just as bad from Nelson's point of view—'

'I'm not taking any action,' Antony pointed out. 'You're assuming that Nelson has been making the telephone calls, then?'

'Nothing else makes sense.'

'No, I'm inclined to agree with you there. But as long as I confine my activities to asking questions I don't see how he can possibly object.'

'In any case,' said Jenny unexpectedly, 'you said yourself, Meg, that things couldn't go on as they are.' She stretched out her hand, and for an instant it closed comfortingly over Meg's. 'Antony knows the score now,' she added. 'You'd better leave the rest to him.'

Meg looked at her in a puzzled way. She didn't seem convinced, but neither did she continue the argument, and she drank up her Dubonnet obediently when Antony reminded her that he hadn't got all day to spend over luncheon.

But neither she nor Jenny had much appetite for the meal.

## II

As for Antony, he went back to chambers fully intending to make the best use of the time which had so unexpectedly been made available to him. He was sorry Meg had been upset, and sorrier still that Jenny was worried; and he took a moment to wonder whether Meg appreciated the real heroism that underlay Jenny's attitude. On second thoughts, he rather thought she did. But one more warning was neither here nor there; he succeeded fairly well in banishing the matter from his mind.

He wasn't interrupted until past five o'clock, when he was on the point of giving up and calling it a day. He had actually got half way round the desk when the telephone rang and he went back to answer it, and there was Hill's voice saying apologetically, 'Someone to see you, Mr Maitland.'

'Tell him I already left.'

'I can't. He—'

'It's late. Won't tomorrow do?'

'—he's here beside me.'

'What?' (Heaven alone knew what Mallory would be thinking of this invasion of his territory. Visitors who knew their place went quietly into the waiting-room.)

'He's—' Hill broke off, and all Antony could hear for a moment was the murmur of voices. 'He says to tell you his name's Nelson,' said Hill, still faintly apologetic, but speaking more loudly than usual, as if there were in the announcement some obscure cause for alarm.

'I see.' It came too pat after his talk with Jenny and Meg to leave him altogether unmoved, but his voice was steady enough. Probably his main emotion was one of amusement. They had all talked glibly about danger, but that could be discounted for the moment at least. A man does not call at chambers of one of the leading criminal lawyers in the country, even to see one of the lesser lights, and send in his name openly, if his immediate intention is criminal. 'If the matter's urgent you'd better tell Mr Nelson to come in,' said Antony, and heard Hill begin to speak, quickly and rather nervously, before the connection was broken.

The man who was shown in by Willett a few moments later was small, probably not more than five foot three. (Willett, who regarded Maitland's affairs as peculiarly his property, looked excited, and closed the door after the visitor had entered with obvious reluctance.) Nelson came across the room slowly; he had an odd, crablike manner of progression ... if you stopped and took careful note you saw that he didn't actually move sideways, but that was the first impression he gave. When he reached the desk he took his time over deciding which was the more comfortable of the two chairs that were placed near it, sat down without invitation, and leaned back, crossing his legs. 'Some dump,' he remarked.

Antony was eyeing him appraisingly. Now that Nelson was seated his lack of inches was not so apparent; he had a large head and a pair of shoulders that might have belonged to a much taller man. As for age, he was probably around fifty. He had black, sleek hair, a good deal of it; a round face with a nose that might once have been broken; thin lips; and brown eyes that seemed to look out at the world with suspicion. He did not seem to like the silence, and when Maitland did not speak immediately he caught his eye and said, 'Well, isn't it?' in a belligerent tone.

It was a narrow room that usually needed the electric light on for the best part of the day. Otherwise, 'It meets my simple needs,' said Antony. He sounded serious enough, but something in his expression must have betrayed him, for Nelson said, in a hectoring way,

'There's nothing to laugh at that I can see.'

'I wasn't exactly laughing,' said Maitland carefully. 'But I think I should point out what one of the clerks should

have told you: that if you want to consult me profession-
ally the approach will have to be made through your
solicitor.'

The other man made a suggestion concerning his solicitor that did not seem to Antony to fall within the realm
of practical politics. 'When I want legal advice I know
where to go for it,' he added. 'This is private, something
between you and me.'

'Are you going to tell me—?'

'Give me time.' He paused, and in his turn seemed
to be assessing his companion. 'You know who I am,' he
said.

'If you are the Nelson who is known to his intimates as
Boney—'

'That's me.' There was no doubt he felt pride in the
sobriquet. 'Bonaparte Nelson. Little and tough ... don't
you make any mistake about that.'

'I'm not likely to,' said Antony fervently. But he was
finding it more and more difficult to believe in the conversation at all.

'That's all right then.' But he was eyeing Maitland brood-
ingly, as though not altogether satisfied with what he saw.
'I've heard of you too. That's why I'm here.'

'At the risk of protracting this conversation unnecessarily,
it might be interesting to know what you have heard.'

'Come off it!' Maitland raised his eyebrows. 'Talk
English!' Boney Nelson exhorted him.

'I think you understood me very well.'

'All right! I've heard that you'll do your best for a chap
that gets himself into trouble. And the cops don't like you
neither.'

'Are you in trouble, Mr Nelson?'

Boney uttered another obscenity. Antony was coming to
the conclusion that his vocabulary was a limited one. 'You
know better than that,' he said then. 'I came to warn you,
that's all.'

'That was kind of you.'

This time Nelson ignored him. 'You and that mate of

yours, Roger Farrell. Be in dead trouble, you will, if you cross me up.'

'If you would tell me how—'

'Don't play the innocent.' The thin lips sneered. 'Got hold of the old man, haven't you? Just a bit too clever!'

'Do you mean Mr Denning?'

'Who do you think I mean? If you'll co-operate, well and good. If not—'

'It would be interesting to know the alternative.'

Boney Nelson made a crude gesture of cutting his throat. 'I don't give no warnings twice,' he said.

'No, I see. But I think in this case you did, didn't you? Once to my wife, and once—only this morning—to Mrs Farrell.'

'I didn't speak to neither of them myself.'

'The calls were made at your instigation,' said Antony, less sure of himself than he sounded. This time Nelson nodded.

'Perhaps,' he said cryptically. His attitude throughout had been vaguely disapproving, but now he relented sufficiently to add, by way of explanation, 'Softening up process. Never underestimate the opposition.'

For some reason, Antony did not find this precept particularly encouraging. 'I've no desire to meddle in your affairs,' he said.

'Tell me another. At any rate, all that can be forgotten ... if you're sensible.'

'Just what do you think I can do for you?'

'I'm offering you a partnership, aren't I?'

'Are you?' said Antony faintly.

'It's not everyone I'd do as much for,' Boney pointed out.

'Just a minute! Did you kill Stoker?'

'What you don't know won't hurt you.'

'I'm really most interested in knowing why.'

'Double-crossing rat,' said Nelson unemotionally. 'Thought he'd get in first with the old man.'

'Who had the key? You—' Nelson shook his head

slightly, a movement which Antony took to be involuntary. 'Your emissary, I should say,' he corrected himself. 'Or Stoker?'

'I suppose they pay you to talk like that.'

'I'm sorry. It's my uncle's influence,' said Antony apologetically.

'Oh, him! Holy terror, isn't he?'

That sounded a promising by-way, but Maitland thought it as well to ignore it. 'Well, if you won't tell me about the key, tell me what would be expected of me as your partner.'

'I'm not suggesting equal shares, mind. But there's a cool million the old man's got salted away. Plenty for all of us.'

'I think I should explain to you that I have very little influence with Mr Denning. As for Farrell, in spite of their relationship—'

'What did he take the old man in for if he isn't going to make something out of it?'

Too difficult to explain. 'Simple human kindness,' said Antony, and Boney snorted his dissatisfaction with the suggestion. 'Believe it or not, neither Farrell nor I has the slightest interest in the gold, except perhaps a certain amount of curiosity as to where it is hidden.'

'Pull the other one!' said Nelson derisively. 'Denning needs help, that's why he's gone to Farrell, and who should *he* ask but you?'

'If I tell you that I hadn't heard of the gold until last Monday, and that Farrell had never heard of it at all until I told him—'

'I wouldn't believe you.'

'You're making things very difficult,' said Maitland, and sighed. 'Anyway, where do I come in?'

'It's no secret that you're a friend of Farrell's, or that he took you to see Denning the day he came out.'

'You're jumping to conclusions, you know. In any case, I don't see why you want our help. Why not approach Mr Denning yourself?'

'He asks me why not! Because I don't want the cops to be as wise as I am, that's why not.'

'Is the house watched?'

'What do you think?'

'All the same—'

'This line you're giving me. How did you know about the gold at all if Denning didn't tell you?'

'Would you consider it indelicate if I mentioned that I had been told of it by the police?'

'Now that,' said Nelson, 'I can't believe.'

'You might have a stab at it,' Maitland suggested. 'It happens to be true, and it would save a good deal of misunderstanding.'

'You're wasting time.'

'Not if I can convince you—'

'Can it. Mind you, I can see your point,' said Boney magnanimously. 'A three-way split—you, and Farrell, and the old man—that's nice work; but not much use to you, because that way you end up dead.'

'Would that do you any good?'

'It might. And then again, it might not. But it's a matter of discipline, see?' said Nelson, making an honest attempt to explain himself. 'There's them as knows I'm after the gold, and if I let you get away with doing me down it might give them ideas.'

'Most undesirable, I can see that,' said Antony seriously. He could see the humour of the situation, with Sir Nicholas's room two doors down the hall, and himself in solemn conclave with a gangster; but he could also see that Boney, having got an idea firmly into his head, wasn't open to the conviction that he was mistaken. And that wasn't funny at all.

'As long as you do. I'd kill you because I'd got to,' said Nelson. If he'd blustered, that might have made it easier to ignore what he was saying. As it was, his whole personality seemed to be behind the words, and it was a cold one.

Antony said, because now it was his turn to be made uneasy by the silence, 'You're offering me an alternative.'

'A bargain,' said Boney, and smiled. It did not, in Maitland's eyes, enhance his charm. 'Find out where the gold is and tell me; you may know where it is already, for all I know.'

'I don't.'

'Find out then,' Boney repeated. 'There'll be twenty thousand in it for each of you ... no, say thirty thousand.' He paused, perhaps in admiration of his own generosity. 'And no risk, not from me, not from the fuzz,' he added. 'Which you shouldn't underestimate, you being an amateur, and all.'

'If I told you that neither Farrell nor I has any interest—'

'Change the record!'

'It's true.'

'Prove it then. Give us the old man.'

'I'm more likely to ask for police protection for him.'

'He wouldn't thank you.'

'I daresay not. All the same—'

Boney Nelson came to his feet. He was suddenly, coldly angry, and when he spoke his tone was vicious. 'I'm warning you,' he said. 'It isn't a game we're playing.'

'If I've given you the impression that I thought it was—'

'I know your kind. Think you're clever, don't you? Well, try and put one over on me and see where it gets you.' He crossed the room to the door and turned there, his hand on the knob, no less impressive for his lack of inches. 'I'll give you till tomorrow to make up your mind,' he said, and pulled the door open.

'I don't—'

'Don't worry, I'll be in touch.' He stood a moment, glaring at Maitland, and then went out, closing the door very gently behind him.

Antony drew a long breath.

## III

He got to the Barhams' house, which was in Wimbledon,

much later than he had intended, but even so Victor Barham had not yet returned from the City. Terry Barham received him in the drawing-room, and David Reade was with her. In fact, he must have heard the bell, for he appeared in the doorway just as a neat maid was letting Maitland into the hall, and he took over convoy duty from her with something of the enthusiasm he had shown two days before. 'This is Antony Maitland, Terry. I told you he'd be coming today.'

Terry was small and inclined to be plump. She had a round, pretty face, and hair that was cut short but still waved wildly about her head. Her eyebrows and lashes were dark, her hair silver-gilt, so that even Antony, who was not particularly observant in these matters, suspected that it owed its colouring to the hairdresser. She was wearing an apple-green dress, for which the room's autumnal shades of decoration were a good background. It was an impeccably kept room, newly furnished in the Scandinavian style ... about as big a contrast as you could imagine to the one at the Reades', but still David looked very much at home in it.

By the time he had observed all this, Antony had crossed the room and taken the hand the girl held out to him. Her greeting was less conventional; she stared up at him wide-eyed for a moment, and then exclaimed ingenuously, 'Good lord, are *you* Antony Maitland,' in a tone that made his murmured, 'I'm afraid so,' sound less banal than it might have done.

'I only meant,' said Terry, 'that I thought you'd be older.' She smiled engagingly, making the words apology and compliment combined. She couldn't have been more than twenty herself; Antony wondered how she had liked the company she had found herself in at the Farrells' two weeks before. Whether she had enjoyed it or not, she now seemed to be enjoying the situation. 'David has told me everything!' she exclaimed, as dramatically as Meg herself might have done.

'Then you know,' said Antony, feeling his way, 'why I'm

here. I was hoping, as perhaps you also know, to see your father as well as you.'

'Daddy won't be long. But it's just as well he isn't here, Mr Maitland, because he'll probably be stuffy about it. He actually *likes* Mr Wilson, you know.'

'I explained,' said David, 'about the key.'

'That was helpful of you,' said Antony dryly. Terry gave another of her abrupt ejaculations.

'Do sit down, both of you,' she said. And when they had obeyed her, 'I'm glad now I went with Daddy. I wouldn't have done if Mother had felt up to it, and I don't mind telling you I thought the evening would be a dead loss, though I *adore* Meg, of course. But I can remember *everything*,' she added triumphantly.

'Then suppose you tell me.' The chair was more comfortable than he had expected from its rather angular lines. 'Did you notice Meg's handbag on the chest on the upstairs landing?'

'Yes, of course I did. It was a marvellous one, really *elegant*, and I decided to look for one just like it, only then I changed my mind because it *is* a little late in the season and though Daddy isn't exactly mean there isn't a hope of getting anything out of him beyond my allowance.'

'The handbag, Terry,' said David, with an apologetic look in Antony's direction.

'Yes, well, it was there when we went upstairs to take our coats off, and it was still there when I went up after dinner. That was after Irene came down ... it's funny she didn't notice it, David.'

'Not so funny. You know Irene, she's always in a dream of some kind.'

'The interesting thing is, who went upstairs after you did, Miss Barham?'

'Mr Wilson went up *just after*,' said Terry, 'and while he was gone Mr Reade went out to fetch his cigars.' She was giving him her full attention now, but even so she was only too obviously aware of David's presence. 'And afterwards Mrs Wilson was upstairs too, and then we all went up together for our coats, and I didn't see the handbag on the chest then.'

'Do you mean it wasn't there, or that you didn't notice either way?'

'I'm afraid I didn't notice, because we were talking, you know. But I do think I would have done, truly. So you see you were quite right in thinking it was *most likely* Mr Wilson.'

'Did David tell you that?'

'Yes. Isn't it true?'

No need to disillusion them. 'I'm not even *sure* that Meg didn't lose the key, or mislay it,' he said evasively, falling unconsciously into Terry's habit of emphasis.

'*Someone* had a key to let that man in,' said Terry. 'And I've been thinking, Mr Maitland,' she added earnestly, 'I used to think Mr Wilson was dull and rather boring, but now I can see that he might easily be *quite sinister*.' She smiled then, seeing his expression, and said without resentment, 'You can laugh at me if you like, but I think you agree with me really.'

'Perhaps I do,' said Antony non-committally. There was a thread of malice in Leonard Wilson's nature that made this not too ridiculous an assertion; but even as he spoke it occurred to him to wonder whether either of these two young people could be quite as artless as they sounded. 'Well, it's no use asking you about Mr Denning's friends—'

'I was fourteen when he went to prison, and I remember him *perfectly*,' said Terry.

'Yes, but you wouldn't be likely to know who he might communicate with when he was coming out,' said David, taking the words out of Antony's mouth. 'And I asked her about the other thing, Mr Maitland, whether she'd talked about that to anybody else, and she hadn't ... only to me.'

'I see. Thank you. Was the subject mentioned between you and your father, Miss Barham, when anybody else might have overheard?'

'No, because Daddy was furious when he heard about Meg and Roger asking Mr Denning to stay with them, and

I didn't want to remind him about it.'

Antony smiled at her. 'You're making me nervous,' he said. 'I gather he's not likely to appreciate my questions.'

'No, and I do feel it's a good thing we could have our talk before he came in. Is that all, Mr Maitland, because if so you'd better have a drink, you may need it.'

It seemed to be a choice between martinis and scotch, so he chose the latter. David went to attend to the matter, again demonstrating the fact that he felt completely at home, and Antony was parrying Terry's questions about a case he had been involved in two years before, which started with a libel action and ended with a murder, when a thought occurred to him and he interrupted her to ask, 'After I phoned you this morning, did you tell your father I was coming?'

For the first time Terry looked a little taken aback. 'Well, no, I didn't,' she admitted. 'You see, now you're here he can't refuse to see you, but if I'd told him he'd have said No, and he wouldn't have let me talk to you either.'

'This way he'll just be furiously angry, he isn't likely to cut me dead,' said Antony. 'You know, you don't comfort me at all.'

Terry laughed, but he was more than half in earnest, and when half past seven came and Victor Barham had still not put in an appearance he was glad enough to take his leave.

## IV

It was a quarter past eight when he let himself into the house in Kempenfeldt Square, too early for Sir Nicholas to be at dinner, but the study door had been left invitingly open. Antony hesitated a moment before he crossed the hall and went in. As he had expected, Sir Nicholas was stretched out at his ease in a chair by the fire, with a glass at his elbow. He did not move immediately, but if his pose was relaxed that was only, Antony felt, the more deceiving.

118

He wasn't surprised to be greeted coldly, and was tempted to reply in kind. Instead he said, mildly.

'I can't really stay, Uncle Nick. Jenny will be waiting.'

'You can give me two minutes of your valuable time,' said Sir Nicholas. 'Long enough to explain the—er—the invasion of chambers this afternoon.'

'That,' said Antony flatly, 'was Boney Nelson.'

'I might have guessed it, I suppose.'

'Well, yes, I think you might. He wasn't there by invitation.'

'I should hope not, indeed.' Sir Nicholas levered himself into a rather more erect position. 'I imagine, however, that your activities were responsible—'

'Perhaps if I'd never gone to see Uncle Hubert ... but I think Nelson would have come to me anyway.'

'What did he want?'

'To offer me thirty thousand pounds,' said Antony, and did not attempt to amplify the statement.

Sir Nicholas compressed his lips, but said only, in an ominously gentle tone, 'For some consideration, no doubt.'

'For telling him where Uncle Hubert has hidden the gold.'

'I see.' He waited a moment, in case his nephew had anything more to say, and then asked, with an edge on his voice, 'Did he by any chance mention what would happen if you did not comply with his request?'

'He said he'd be in touch with me tomorrow.'

'That doesn't—'

'No, I know, Uncle Nick. He said his reputation wouldn't stand being done down by amateurs.'

'And so?'

'He threatened to kill me.'

Sir Nicholas did not comment on that for a moment, then he said icily, 'You meant to keep that from me.'

'This is the first chance I've had—'

'Perhaps it is. But it is not the first you have heard from this Boney Nelson, is it?' He pronounced the name wryly, as though it had a bitter taste.

'You mean the telephone call the other night?'

'Precisely. Jenny knew who it was from.'

'At that point neither of us did. I only found out this afternoon that it wasn't Nelson after all, but one of his minions. Anyway, he never spoke to me, and when he spoke to Jenny he made no specific threat.'

'You'll go to the police, of course.'

'That's changing your tune, Uncle Nick. Only two days ago—'

'The circumstances have altered.'

Sir Nicholas was in no mood to be satisfied by a quibble. Recognising this, Antony said, 'I'll talk to Sykes, of course.' And then, though he realised the futility of appeasement at this stage, 'I did my best to persuade Nelson that I had no interest in the gold.'

'I am glad you showed so much good sense,' said his uncle, in his most crushing tone. 'The point is, did you succeed?'

'I can't say that I did.'

'If you had not this passion for involving yourself with the underworld—'

'Uncle Nick, you said yourself I had to do what I could for Roger.'

'Certainly I did. But can you tell me that, if you had not already acquired a reputation for meddling, any of this would have happened?'

'No, I can't honestly say that,' said Antony, depressed.

Unexpectedly, Sir Nicholas smiled at him. 'Well, we must see what Sykes has to say,' he remarked. Antony was used to his uncle's swift changes of mood, but even so he felt surprised by the cordiality of his tone. 'In the meantime, you will oblige me by taking care.'

'I shall do that all right.'

'And see that Jenny does the same.'

'You don't have to tell me.'

'No, I'm sorry.' The apology was almost unprecedented. 'Have your researches so far borne fruit?' asked Sir Nicholas, still amiably.

'I've seen the Wilsons, and Terry Barham. Not her father yet.'

'And—?'

'As far as I can see any of them could have taken the key, except perhaps Victor Barham. And I suppose we have to admit the possibility that he might have got it through Terry.'

'Do you really think that is likely?'

'None of it is *likely*, Uncle Nick.'

'I suppose not.' Sir Nicholas sounded dissatisfied.

Antony waited to see if he had anything to add to that. 'I ought to go,' he said.

'You'll get in touch with Sykes.'

'Tomorrow morning, first thing.'

'Why not tonight?'

'I want to see Uncle Hubert again.'

'That,' said Sir Nicholas, with more energy than he had so far displayed, 'would be most unwise.'

'Do you think so?'

'I do!'

'No, but look here, Uncle Nick, he's nearly eighty. If he isn't willing to take on Boney Nelson for possession of the gold he may be persuaded to tell the police where it is.'

'Do you think there is any likelihood of that?'

'It's worth trying.'

'Very well.' He raised his voice a little as his nephew started to move towards the door. 'I shall rely on you, Antony,' he said, in the tone of one who will stand no nonsense, 'to keep me informed.'


V


Over dinner Antony did his best to impress upon Jenny the need for caution, without alarming her unduly about Boney Nelson's threats. He couldn't congratulate himself on having much success. Jenny gave him one of her clear-eyed looks and said positively, 'It's much more likely that he'll try to harm you.'

'I'll take care, love, don't worry.'

Jenny smiled at that. 'I don't see how I can help it,' she said. 'But there's nothing to be done, is there? I mean, you can't let Roger down.'

'No, I can't. I don't even want to,' he admitted. 'I shall tell Sykes what happened, of course.'

'Of course,' Jenny echoed, and went on with her dinner in silence for a while. He had almost forgotten what they had been talking about when she said suddenly, 'Do you think it will do any good?'

'What? Oh, telling Sykes. I don't know, love, we shall just have to wait and see.'

'It would show your good faith, wouldn't it? Yours and Roger's.'

'It might.'

'You don't sound very sure about that.'

'I'm not sure about anything,' said Antony disconsolately. And then, with more energy, 'Except that I want to see Uncle Hubert again this evening. Is Roger coming here?'

'He rang up about six o'clock to say he'd be in later. Can I come too?'

'Not this time, I think, Jenny. It's time for some plain speaking.'

He thought she would argue about that, but she said only, 'I see,' and took away his empty plate and pushed the cheese towards him. After a time she said philosophically, 'I suppose you'll tell me what happens when you get home. Which is more than you did about your talk with Boney Nelson, isn't it?'

He was still protesting that he had been completely candid with her when Roger arrived. Somehow he wasn't left with the feeling that he had been altogether convincing.

# VI

Roger had his car with him that evening, and they left almost immediately. It wasn't far to Beaton Street, and Antony occupied the time by giving his friend a brief run down of the day's events. 'I needn't tell you,' he added, as Roger brought the car smoothly into the kerb, 'that it means you and Meg will have to take care too.'

'I'm almost tempted,' said Roger, still staring straight ahead through the windscreen, 'to do what he asks.'

'We don't know where the gold is,' Antony pointed out.

'I didn't mean that. Obviously if we did know we'd have to tell the police. But Uncle Hubert ... he's safe enough, I suppose, while he stays here and the police are keeping an eye on the house. But if I told him he'd have to go to an hotel—'

'Boney Nelson would have whisked him away in a plain van before you could count a hundred.'

'And after that he might leave us alone.' Roger sighed. 'Oh, well, it's an academic question anyway. I couldn't square it with my conscience.' But there was a grim look about his mouth when he turned for the first time to look directly at Antony. 'Shall we go in?' he said.

Since he last saw it, it seemed to Maitland that there had been some subtle change in the Farrells' living-room. It looked tidier, more polished, as if Hubert Denning's personality had in some way stamped itself on his surroundings. The old man was sitting in the same arm-chair, completely at his ease. He looked up with a smile as they went in, but when he saw Antony his eyes became wary. His tone, however, was genial. 'My friend Mr Maitland,' he said.

Antony said, 'Good evening,' and was amused as he said it to hear the conventional politeness in his tone. He went across the room and took the chair that Jenny had sat in the last time they were there.

'Your charming wife isn't with you?' Denning asked.

'Not today.'

'The fact is,' said Roger, with the abruptness that always seemed to affect him in his godfather's presence, 'we both feel it's time for a little straight talk with you.'

'You alarm me,' said Hubert Denning placidly. He looked and sounded amused. 'Meanwhile, I hope you will observe, Roger, that my glass is empty. And you haven't offered our guest a drink.'

Roger gave a wordless exclamation that conveyed his feelings accurately enough. He fetched the decanter in silence and refilled the old man's glass; poured whisky generously for Antony, and nearly as generously for himself; added water to both glasses and brought them across the room with him, putting them down on the table at Antony's elbow; pulled forward the sofa until it was directly opposite the fire, and equidistant from both his companions. The room began to feel a little more like itself.

'You'd better tell him, Antony,' said Roger, still abruptly.

'Very well.' He wasn't in any hurry to begin. He sipped his whisky and kept his eyes fixed on Uncle Hubert's face; but if he hoped to detect some sign of uneasiness he was disappointed. 'I'll begin by saying, Mr Denning, that I don't believe you told us the truth the other night.'

'I don't recall—' He appealed to Roger. 'Did I tell you anything?' he asked. But it was Antony who replied.

'Two negative statements,' he said. 'You hadn't been in touch with William Stoker, and nobody—besides ourselves and the authorities, knew when you were coming out of prison.'

'That is correct.'

'I ought to tell you that I had a visit from Boney Nelson today.'

'Am I supposed to know this—this rather oddly-named individual?'

'In case you don't, he's a gangster with a reputation for meanness and brutality, according to my friend, Chief Inspector Sykes. Stoker joined his mob after you went to prison.'

'This passion for calling a spade a spade, Mr Maitland—'

'Let's say, then, after you retired, temporarily, from the public gaze. Nelson more or less admitted to me that Stoker had died because he had double-crossed him.'

'What is that to do with me?'

'I'll tell you what I think happened, if you like. I think you got in touch with Stoker while you were still inside—'

'How could I do that?'

'I don't know. I only know it *can* be done. You wanted his help in getting hold of the gold you have hidden—'

'Good heavens, Mr Maitland, what a lurid imagination you have. But I interrupted you,' said Uncle Hubert remorsefully. 'Please go on with what you were saying.'

'You got in touch with him, you wanted his help. He decided to go it alone, without reference to Boney Nelson, but somehow Nelson got wind of what was happening ... probably from the two other members of your crew who are now his henchmen. He made it his business to get hold of a key to this house—'

'Why should he do that, I wonder?'

'At a guess, he had some idea of putting pressure on you through Roger. He couldn't, at that stage, have known that you were coming to stay here, but when he did know it must have confirmed him in his belief—which unfortunately the police share—that there was some sort of unholy alliance between you.'

'What a lot you have learned since last we spoke together,' Hubert Denning marvelled.

'Haven't I? But to go back to what I think happened the night Stoker died. Somehow or other he mistook the day you would be coming here, and turned up on the doorstep on the evening of the fifteenth. Nelson had him followed, suspecting a double-cross ... he may even have followed him himself. What he saw confirmed his suspicions, he held Stoker up on the doorstep, opened the door and forced him to come into the house, and killed him in the hall.'

'I have always admired your ingenuity, Mr Maitland,' said Uncle Hubert gently.

'If you can explain what happened any other way—'

'I won't even try. There was some mix up at first about the date I was coming home,' the old man admitted. 'If Stoker had heard something, through some of these mysterious channels of yours, it all might have fallen out as you surmise.'

'But you didn't get in touch with him?'

'No.' He held up a restraining hand when Antony was about to speak again. 'I do not deny the existence of a quantity of gold, since you seem to know so much. But at my time of life I have really no interest in such mundane matters any longer.'

'Then you won't mind telling the police where it is.'

'But I do mind, very much. The police are no doubt an admirable body of men, but I have no particular regard for them.'

'It wouldn't be to *their* benefit. The insurance company, I suppose—'

Hubert Denning shook his head regretfully. 'There has been enough trouble about that gold,' he said. 'Let it lie where it is.'

'Boney Nelson is after it,' said Roger.

'That does not concern me.'

'It will if he gets his hands on you,' said Roger bluntly.

'I cannot believe there is the least danger of that. It may have escaped your notice, my boy, but the house is under observation by the police, and on my walks I have been accompanied—'

'I can see,' said Antony, 'that I shall have to be even more frank with you, Mr Denning. Unfortunately, both the police and Boney Nelson believe that Roger is venal, that he is willing to help you obtain possession of the gold. Nelson believes that I, too, am part of the conspiracy. He has made certain threats—'

'I am beginning to see where this is leading. But that, too, Mr Maitland, is no concern of mine.'

'You may not care much what happens to me, or to Roger. But what about Jenny and Meg?'

'Did he threaten to harm them?'

'Not specifically. But it is inherent in the situation—'

'I think you are giving way to your fears too readily, Mr Maitland. Roger, I should have thought, would have more sense.' There was a coldness in his tone that reminded Antony, only too vividly, of their last meeting, seven years ago.

'You can't stay here for ever,' said Roger, with a helpless look in Antony's direction.

'I feel sure there will be no need for that,' said Hubert Denning, benevolent once again. 'Meg will find me a *pied-à-terre*, and by that time both the police and Boney Nelson will have lost interest in the gold.'

'But if you've no interest in it yourself, why the bloody hell won't you tell us where it is and get it over with?'

'May I remind you, Roger, that I have the greatest dislike for intemperate language. I have told you I intend to take no action in the matter. I must ask you to leave it at that.'

And though they argued with him, in turns and both together, for the best part of an hour, that was all the satisfaction they got.

I

Chief Inspector Sykes wasn't available until eleven o'clock the next morning, and then he wouldn't have time to come to the cafe where they had had their previous meeting. Antony was restless until it was time to leave for his appointment at New Scotland Yard, and didn't feel that what should have been a useful interlude at his desk had really done much good. To add to his annoyance he found himself short of time after all, and had to take a taxi, instead of walking at least part of the way, by which means he might have shaken off some of his ill humour.

The detective listened in silence to what he had to say, outwardly as placid as usual, but inwardly Antony sensed that he was perturbed. 'I warned you, Mr Maitland,' he said, when the story was finished.

'So you did. And if you think that's any better than saying "I told you so"—'

Sykes ignored the protest, which indeed was somewhat half-hearted. 'May I ask you one thing? What did your friend, Mr Farrell, have to say when you told him about Boney Nelson's visit?'

'He agreed that I should see you as soon as possible.'

'But all the same you waited until this morning—'

'That was my idea. I wanted to talk to Hubert Denning first. And as you seem to be still suspicious of Roger's motives, may *I* remind *you*, Chief Inspector, that Boney Nelson more or less admitted responsibility for William Stoker's death.'

'You wouldn't get very far with that story in a court of law.'

'Don't I know it?'

'Nor do I think that Chief Superintendent Briggs will find it convincing.'

'I suppose you have to drag Briggs into it.'

'You know perfectly well, Mr Maitland, that he is in charge of the case.'

'Yes, I know. You told me that too.'

'What was the upshot of your talk with Mr Denning?'

'He professed to have no further interest in the gold, which I take leave to doubt, but refused to tell you people where it is hidden. He also denied that he had been in touch with Stoker about its recovery, but I don't think I believe him about that either. Boney Nelson talked about double-crossing ... but I told you that.'

'You say Nelson is going to get in touch with you again today.'

'That's what he said.'

'And you'll tell him—?'

'I'll try again to convince him that Roger and I have no interest in the gold, but I don't somehow think I shall succeed. I needn't tell you that what I'm worried about is Jenny's safety, and Meg's.'

'I can arrange for them to receive police protection.'

'Would Briggs agree to that, if he doesn't believe in the threat?'

'I think I can convince him—' But before he had time to finish Antony broke in bitterly.

'I suppose your offer includes us ... Roger and me. It would provide an excellent excuse to keep us under observation without any further complaint. At least you'll admit that if we had any nefarious intentions the story I've told you this morning is the last one I'd have dreamed up.'

'I'm quite sure you would foresee the consequences. But, Mr Maitland, I have never had any doubt of *your* good intentions.'

'Roger agreed to my suggestion.'

'It could be said that he wants to work behind a screen of police activity,' said Sykes bluntly. 'But, in any case, could he have done anything else without forfeiting your good opinion?'

'You forget, Chief Inspector, *I* have no doubts of his honesty. If he'd put up an argument I expect I'd have listened to him.'

'I've no doubt you think you're telling me the truth, Mr Maitland, but I wonder if you're really right about that.'

'Oh, w-what's the use?' said Antony, his irritation getting the better of him. 'If you're going to twist everything I say—'

'Would you like to tell the Chief Superintendent the story yourself?' Sykes suggested.

'Would I ... h-hell!' Antony came to his feet with a violent movement. 'I thought you'd h-have more s-sympathy with the p-problem,' he said.

'I understand your anxiety about Mrs Maitland's safety, and Mrs Farrell's. We'll do our best for them, but I wish I could make you see the matter from our point of view.'

'You can try,' said Antony grimly.

'It is possible—you must admit it's possible—that Mr Denning or Mr Farrell will themselves be in touch with Boney Nelson.'

'Denning perhaps ... not R-roger.'

'Such an action,' said Sykes imperviously, 'would meet Nelson's demands. It is unlikely that under those circumstances he would interfere any further with you.'

'Yes, I see that. But Uncle Hubert ... he'd want more than the thirty thousand Nelson is offering.'

'You think he is after the gold himself ... the full amount?'

'Yes, I do. He's an old hypocrite, and when he says there's been enough trouble about the gold and he intends to take no further action about it, I'm pretty sure he's lying.'

'He himself is under observation, Mr Maitland.'

'So he told me. But you can't keep tabs on him for ever. He pointed that out too.'

Sykes got up, more slowly than Antony had done. 'I can only ask you to leave the matter in our hands,' he said.

Antony turned and made for the door without another word, but he paused when he got there. 'Tt-thank you, Ch-chief Inspector,' he said ironically, and was gone.


## II

He had lunch with Sir Nicholas, and dwelt at length upon his grievance. 'I don't know what you're complaining about,' his uncle said at length, losing patience. 'Police surveillance won't cramp your activities at all, or Roger's.'

'But they're providing it for the wrong reason. Even in my case ... Sykes may believe me, but I bet Briggs doesn't.'

'If you are going to allow that to worry you—'

'It d-doesn't. It only annoys me,' said Antony, with a dignity that was only partly spoiled by the stammer that had crept into his voice again. Sir Nicholas looked at him coldly.

'There is never anything gained by losing your temper,' he pointed out. And then, taking the initiative into his own hands, 'In many ways I find your own conduct as stupid as Roger's has been.'

That at least had the advantage of distracting Antony from his previous complaint. He spent the next ten minutes explaining how perfectly rational everything he had done had been.


## III

He had never been less in the mood for work. He wasn't in the mood for interviewing Victor Barham either, but he thought perhaps that was the lesser of two evils. Anyway, he had made an appointment with the great man's secretary earlier in the day, and so was more or less committed.

The Imperial Insurance Company occupied a building of some magnificence, which had been new when he had

had occasion to visit it some six or seven years before, but he knew from experience that not all its occupants were equally magnificently housed. That didn't apply to the Managing Director though; he had a sort of penthouse suite, reached only by a private and very luxurious lift, and even then you had to make your approach through several ranks of underlings before you reached the presence. Antony, who was still feeling irritable, remained unawed, but thought fit to assume a conciliatory attitude when he finally gained his objective, particularly as Barham greeted him with a severe, unsmiling look.

'You intimated to my secretary, Mr Maitland, that you wished to see me on a matter of some importance. I hope she did not misunderstand you.' He was a little man, very erect and dignified, with iron-grey hair, brown eyes like his daughter's and impeccable tailoring.

Antony said diffidently, 'It was a little difficult to explain my errand, except personally to you.'

'Indeed? Well, you had better sit down.'

'Thank you.' The chair was comfortable. He wished his host's manner reflected this characteristic. 'There are a few questions I should like to ask you, if you will permit me.'

'Questions! What questions?'

'I'm a friend of Meg and Roger Farrell.' He paused a moment, hoping that might elicit some more encouraging response. 'You visited them one Sunday evening, nearly a fortnight ago now.'

'Certainly I did. I and my daughter, Teresa.'

He was conscious of a firm conviction that it wouldn't be a popular move to say he had seen Terry already. 'That evening you heard, I believe for the first time, that Hubert Denning was coming out of prison the following week. My first question is whether you mentioned that fact to anyone at all.'

'There was some discussion about it at the dinner table. You know, I suppose, that he is Roger's godfather, and that Roger had suggested putting him up.'

'I believe the suggestion came from the prison chaplain actually,' said Antony, still apologetic.

'No matter. I told Roger what I thought of his foolishness, and that I hoped he would attempt no contact with my family while the old man remained under his roof. Is that why—I don't see the connection—but is that why you are here today?'

'A man was killed in the Farrells' house ... you must have read about it in the papers.'

Barham inclined his head, but his tone remained as stiff as ever. 'That does not concern me,' he said.

'But it may concern Uncle Hubert—Mr Denning,' he corrected himself. 'The man who was killed was a former associate of his.' He went on quickly, before the other man could protest. 'That's why I wanted to know if you had told anybody ... anybody at all—'

'I should not dream of discussing Roger's affairs, particularly anything so unpleasant, even with my wife.'

If Antony thought for a moment, What a dull life you must lead, he allowed no flicker of emotion to disturb his earnestness. 'You might have mentioned the matter to one of your colleagues. After all, Denning was one of your Directors, wasn't he?'

'The connection was severed years ago.'

'Of course. But—'

'I have no time for gossip ... for unsavoury gossip, at that.' He began to get up as he spoke, but sat down again when he saw that Antony did not follow his example. 'Mr Maitland, I really must ask you—'

'There is one more question, Mr Barham.'

'I cannot see why I should submit to this—this inquisition.'

'Out of friendship for Roger perhaps.'

'Are you telling me that the police suspect he had something to do with that man's death?'

'The police,' said Antony, sighing, 'have notoriously suspicious minds.'

'Then I cannot see ... really, Mr Maitland, you must

have a very odd idea of me if you think I have any intention of concerning myself in such an unpleasant affair.' This time he came all the way to his feet. Antony followed suit more slowly. Barham's mouth was set in an implacable line that he didn't like at all; it augured ill for his mission.

'You won't even hear my question?' he asked.

'I will not.' There must have been a concealed bell-push, for the door opened at that moment and the secretary came in ... a middle-aged woman, as neat in her own large way as her employer. 'Mr Maitland is leaving now,' said Victor Barham.

It seemed a long way to the door.


IV

When he thought it over, it didn't seem to matter so much. Victor Barham had given him food for thought, if nothing else. So Maitland went back to chambers and occupied himself with a new set of papers that old Mr Mallory had accepted on his behalf; though, as the case wasn't likely to come on before the next session, there didn't seem to be any great urgency about them.

Boney Nelson didn't make the expected telephone call until nearly ten o'clock that evening, by which time both Sir Nicholas and Roger had joined the Maitlands' vigil. There had been several false alarms already, so that now Antony was almost surprised when he picked up the receiver and heard the familiar, rather grating voice. 'Said I'd be in touch, didn't I?' said Boney Nelson.

Antony found that his mouth was dry. He turned his back on the room, knowing the others were listening. He said, as naturally as he could, 'I've been waiting for your call,' and heard Jenny catch her breath sharply, and then let it out again in a long sigh. Sir Nicholas muttered something that was probably meant to be reassuring, but he couldn't quite catch what it was. Roger got up quietly;

134

he could tell because the springs at that end of the sofa creaked. Boney Nelson's voice said harshly in his ear,

'Have you thought about my proposition?'

The answer to that was, of course, that he'd thought about nothing else all day. He said, carefully, 'In the circumstances, as I outlined them to you, there's nothing to think about.'

'You wouldn't still be trying to have me on, would you?' The rough tone was menacing now.

'I might be, if I thought I could get away with it,' said Antony, more lightly than he felt. For some reason, Nelson seemed to find this encouraging.

'That's better,' he said. 'You're ready to do a deal.'

'I'm not in a position to ... I told you that. Even if I wanted to, I'm not in Denning's confidence.'

'You went to see him last night.'

'To try to persuade him to talk to the police.'

'Don't give me that!'

'I haven't anything else to give you.' That was greeted with silence, so he went on after a brief pause, 'If you know so much you probably know that I went to Scotland Yard this morning.'

He hadn't known. There was another silence, not so long as the last, and then Boney Nelson said angrily, 'Asking for trouble, aren't you?'

'Not exactly. I'm trying to convince you that I can't help you, even if I wanted to.'

'Have you talked to Farrell?'

'Yes, of course. He's of the same mind as I am.'

That, too, was followed by silence. After a long moment Boney Nelson laughed and replaced the receiver with a jarring crash.

They discussed it, of course, until it was time for Roger to leave to collect Meg from the theatre. Antony tried to be reassuring, but it was a waste of time really; somehow none of them felt convinced by his determined cheerfulness.

'There's nothing any of you can do in face of this unreasonable attitude,' said Sir Nicholas, summing the matter up, 'except to exercise the most extreme caution.'

'The police—' said Antony, but his uncle took him up quickly.

'*Extreme* caution,' he repeated gently, and Antony, recognising the danger signal, left it at that.

# Saturday, 25th April

## I

Saturday turned out to be one of those rare, mild April mornings that make you glad to be alive. Jenny and Antony walked in the park, accompanied at a discreet interval by two plain-clothes men, and returned home at about noon with a good appetite for lunch ... which, according to custom, they would be taking with Sir Nicholas. Jenny was wrestling with her hair, trying to make it look less windswept, when the phone rang; but Antony was in the living-room, so it seemed unreasonable to expect her to take the call. When he lifted the receiver he was greeted by Roger's voice, a trifle querulous. 'I've been trying to get you for hours.'

'Well, I'm sorry I ... *what's happened?*'

'Nothing to get excited about,' said Roger soothingly; and that was unreasonable, if you liked. 'I had a call from the constable at Grunning's Hole. He says somebody broke into the cottage and ransacked it pretty thoroughly, and I wondered ... do you think it was a coincidence, it happening just now?'

'No,' said Antony positively. And then, after a moment's thought, 'You told me once the *Susannah* had moorings in the Blackwater.'

'She used to lie in Salley Basin, that's on the north bank.'

'How far would that be from Grunning's Hole?'

'I'd have to look at a map.'

'Look at one then.'

'All right.' After an interval he came back to the telephone, and Antony could hear him muttering to himself before he said, in a tone that was suddenly more alert,

'Not more than about ten miles as the crow flies. I could have sworn—'

'And if you don't happen to be a crow?'

Roger was muttering again, a bit more intelligibly this time. 'You'd have to get across the Colne. There's a C road up to B1026, you'd have to go through Tolleshunt D'Arcy, then across country again to Wivenhoe ... not more than about twenty miles, all told.'

'Then you can see the argument, can't you? If you had been in with Uncle Hubert all along—'

'You think they were looking for the gold?'

'What else?'

'Boney Nelson and company?'

'I imagine so. Or ... have you told Uncle Hubert?'

'Yes, I have. He said, "Tut"—I didn't know anybody really said that—and then told me that we must take the rough with the smooth in this imperfect world.'

'You don't think he might really have used Grunning's Hole for a hiding place?'

'He didn't seem at all disturbed by what I told him.'

'No, but—'

'I want to go down there, Antony. Meg's upset at what has happened.'

'Well, all right. There's no reason why we shouldn't go, and it mightn't be a bad idea to tell Sykes what has happened.'

'I'll leave that to you. When can you be ready?'

'Two o'clock, if I don't want to give Uncle Nick indigestion by rushing through my lunch.'

'We'll have to stay the night. Do you think ... it might be a good idea if Jenny stayed with Meg. I'd suggest the other way around, only I suppose we can't very well leave Uncle Hubert to fend for himself.'

'I can't see that it would do him the least harm, but Jenny will be glad of the company, I expect. I'll ring off now, Roger, and brief the police on what's happening. At least they won't be able to complain of lack of co-operation.'

But he sat for nearly five minutes before he took up the

receiver again, and made a whole series of illegible notes on the pad that lay handy on the writing-table.


## II


The village of Grunning's Hole straggled along one bank of the creek, a single row of cottages facing the hard. The Farrells' cottage was larger than the rest, a detached building about five hundred yards to the east of its nearest neighbour. From what Meg had said it had been pretty bleak and uncomfortable before her marriage to Roger, but since then it had been made over to her specifications and boasted such luxuries as a bathroom, a modernised kitchen, Dunlopillo mattresses, and armchairs that could only be regarded as an encouragement to sinful sloth. Antony, of course, who had stayed there many times, was perfectly familiar with all this, but even the police report of what had happened had not prepared him for the disorder that met his eyes when Roger pushed open the door.

It led straight into the living-room, which was large enough to have been two rooms originally, but had a rather low, heavily raftered ceiling, the centre beam probably not more than eight feet from the floor. And when you looked again, there was a mad sort of order about the chaos. The carpet had been taken up, all the pictures removed from the walls (some rather bad prints, of the sort usually found in the dining-rooms of country hotels, to which Roger was inexplicably attached) and roughly stacked on the sofa, the ashes raked out of the grate, and all the furniture moved around so that it now stood huddled in the centre of the room. 'It *was* the gold they were looking for,' said Antony, following Roger in and closing the door behind him.

Roger took a little longer to weigh up the scene. 'Something large, certainly,' he said then. 'Nothing that could have been stuffed inside a cushion, for instance, or hidden in the upholstery of a chair.'

'For which we may be thankful. It shouldn't take too much doing to restore the *status quo*. They looked for signs that the walls had been tampered with, or the floor taken up, or something buried under the hearth. I suppose the rest of the place—'

'We'd better look.' They went through the rooms rapidly —kitchen, bathroom, and two bedrooms upstairs—and everything they saw confirmed that first impression. 'Did you tell the local constabulary what time we should arrive?' said Antony as they came back to the living-room again.

'I said about half past five.' Roger glanced at his watch. 'We made better time than I expected, but I daresay he—it's just one chap—saw the car coming through the village.'

Antony thought, but did not say, that it would have been strange if he hadn't. The Jensen was nothing if not noticeable. He said, vaguely, 'I expect he'll be along then,' because he was still mentally cataloguing the signs of the search that had gone on.

Roger went across to the window, and stood looking across the narrow road, that came to a dead end a few yards past his gate, to the grey waters of the creek. He seemed to be tired, a condition almost unknown to him, and there was a look of strain about his eyes. He said, after a rather lengthy pause, and without turning his head, 'What did Sykes say when you told him?'

If Antony thought the question should have been asked before, he didn't say so. He had been aware of his friend's preoccupation, ever since Roger had picked him up in Kempenfeldt Square after lunch, and hadn't particularly wanted to intrude on it. 'He was ... noncommittal,' he said, taking his time to choose the word he wanted. 'When I told him we were coming down here he asked if we wanted our police protection to be continued, and I said, No. I take it that was right?'

'It couldn't matter less,' said Roger, too emphatically.

'I was thinking of your local reputation.' He tried for a light tone, but didn't quite achieve it. 'Something's bothering you,' he said then. 'Has anything happened that I don't know about?'

'Nothing. Nothing at all.'

'You might as well tell me,' said Antony, ignoring the denial.

'Well, if you must know'—Roger sounded unaccountably surly—'I don't see the end of all this.'

First he had had to reassure Meg, and now it was her husband's turn. 'You're thinking the whole thing may peter out without ever reaching a crisis. I wish *I* thought so.'

Roger smiled, but the smile did not touch his eyes. 'You're being very forbearing, Antony, not saying "I told you so", when I know I brought the whole thing on myself by agreeing to take in Uncle Hubert; but I'm quite aware of what the police must think ... and other people too, for all I know.'

'As you knew about the police attitude already,' said Antony carefully, 'I take it it's the "other people" who are bothering you. Who, for instance? Is it any use saying, they're not worth worrying about?'

Roger ignored this. 'You seem to trust me—'

'Don't be a fool!'

'—though I don't know why you should. But how do I know about Jenny ... any of the people I care about?' He paused, and then added painfully, 'Even ... Meg.'

'Now that,' said Antony, sitting down rather suddenly on the arm of a chair that happened to be handy, 'is the craziest thing I ever heard you say.'

'Do you think so?' Roger turned from the window, and for the first time looked at his companion squarely. 'Seven years ago, when the police were all set to arrest me for the murder of Martin Grainger, I'm not at all sure that Meg didn't entertain some doubts herself.'

'Even if that were true, and I'm pretty sure it isn't,' said Antony, uttering the lie without a qualm, 'there's a good deal of difference between wondering whether you might have killed a blackmailer who was responsible for the death of your mother, and thinking you might be master-minding a particularly bloody-minded gang.'

'I suppose so,' said Roger hopefully. 'Then you don't think—?'

'Has Meg ever given you the slightest reason—?'

'Not really. I'm not in any doubt that she loves me, you know,' said Roger, turning back to the window again, and Antony spared a moment to reflect that of all his friends Farrell was the only one who could have made a remark like that so simply, 'but she has been pretty depressed.'

'Can you give me one good reason why she shouldn't be?'

'I suppose—'

'You needn't worry, anyway. What does all this mean' —he waved a hand to indicate the disorder around them —'if not that Boney Nelson has every intention of forcing a crisis if necessary? And that's a thought, Roger. I wonder if he knows something we don't.'

'How could he?'

'From Uncle Hubert's former "employees".'

'But if they know—'

'They might just have suspected that he was up to something down here, and for all we know they may have been right. As you pointed out yourself, Grunning's Hole isn't very far from the mooring the old boy kept on the Black-water.'

'But ... where then?' said Roger, looking around him rather wildly.

'I haven't the faintest idea. But it's worth considering... don't you think?'

'I daresay it is,' said Roger rather grudgingly, 'but I don't see how it helps us at all.'

'I have an idea about that. What did Uncle Hubert say when you told him you were coming down here?'

'I told you.'

'Yes, I know. Some sanctimonious drivel about taking the rough with the smooth. You also said he didn't seem at all put out, but—'

'Well?'

'I have an idea his patience may not be inexhaustible. If he gets the idea that Boney Nelson is getting "warm" in his search—'

'You're saying he may make a move himself.'

'Why not?'

'He couldn't act alone. Really, Antony, can you see a man of eighty shifting that quantity of bullion single-handed?'

'It was only an idea.'

Something in Roger's tone prompted him to speak placatingly, but he wasn't surprised when his friend said impatiently, 'We may as well confine ourselves to what's practical.'

'Yes, of course.'

'Then—' He broke off, and changed the course of his remarks. 'Here's Mason now.'

'The local bobby?'

'That's right. I don't suppose he can tell us anything we don't know.'

'No. I imagine he's here to ask questions, not to answer them. But do you think there's any point in confusing him with facts?'

Roger had a brief, amused look for that, but still he protested, 'Sykes already knows—'

'Yes, but he wasn't impressed by the possibilities. Even if they were approached I think Scotland Yard's view would be that the affair was purely local.'

'But as far as I can see nothing has been taken.'

'Vandalism, then. It's never any good arguing with the police, Roger. You can't win.'

Constable Mason, while this exchange had been going on, had leaned his bicycle against the gate-post and proceeded up the path to the front door. He was the stolid, rather slow-spoken type of countryman whom town dwellers are apt to put down without further thought as being slow-witted. Neither Antony, who was meeting him for the first time, nor Roger, who over the years had grown to know him well, was in danger of making that mistake, and Antony at least was relieved that he appeared perfectly content with the answers that Roger gave him. He had ideas of his own about whom the vandals might be ... local youths who were ripe for any mischief. They didn't try to disabuse his mind of the idea.

After he had gone they set about putting the place to rights. According to Mason, Mrs Carter, the village woman who obliged the Farrells, and whose routine visit to air the cottage had resulted in the alarm being given in the first place, had had to be prevented, almost by force, from tackling the job single handed; but most of the furniture was old-fashioned and heavy, and they were both out of breath and sweating by the time order reigned once more.

So they showered, and Roger phoned Meg, who was no more temperamental than the next woman, but—perhaps because her nerves were already stretched unduly—had taken the ransacking of the cottage hard and was now in need of reassurance. By the time Roger replaced the receiver Antony was already aware of hunger. 'We ought to have told them to expect us at the *Cross Keys*,' he said.

Roger smiled at him. He seemed more at ease now, perhaps the job requiring physical effort had been good for him. 'Don't worry,' he said. 'P.C. Mason wouldn't be the only one who noticed our arrival. They'll have something ready for us.'

'Then I vote we don't keep them waiting.' He turned down the lamp on the sideboard until no more than a glimmer of light was left. 'How is Meg?' he asked.

'All right, now she knows nothing was really damaged. For some reason she likes this place.'

'Which is just as well, considering your own predilection for it.'

The *Cross Keys* stood half way along the village street, at the bottom of the short lane that led to the church. The inn was a solid, rather ugly building with a garish sign, but cosy enough inside. As Roger had surmised, they were obviously expected; Simms, the innkeeper, greeted them both by name and regaled them with steak and kidney pie and a good cheese to follow in a dark corner of the private bar. By the time they had finished the meal he was back behind the bar again, and the room had filled up. There was a haze of smoke over everything and a comfortable murmur of talk. Roger watched the last of their supper dishes being removed, and then made his way to the bar for two fresh tankards of beer; as he reached his objective there came a moment of silence, so that Antony could hear the publican's question quite clearly. 'We was all sorry to hear what had happened at your London house last week, Mr Farrell.' (Of course, Meg was well known in the village, and the information in the press that Margaret Hamilton's house had been the scene of a murder meant more to the inhabitants than it would, for instance, to the average theatre-goer.) 'Have the police found out yet who did it?'

'Not yet.' There was obviously, Antony thought, no malice in the question, but the soft murmur of acquiescence that followed indicated too great an interest for comfort, and Roger's tone wasn't altogether easy. He added, turning a little so that his answer was addressed to the room in general, not just to the man behind the bar, 'As to whether they've found out anything, I'm not in their confidence, I'm afraid.'

'Acourse not.' That was Simms again, a little put out by the general interest his remarks had aroused. 'Someone who broke in, the papers said.'

'Yes, obviously.'

'And now,' said a big man sitting in a favoured corner near the fire, 'they've broken in on you down here too.' He paused to puff at a singularly malodorous pipe, and then to refresh himself from the pint-pot at his elbow. 'The same ones, do you reckon?'

'I don't know,' said Roger lamely, but the words seemed in some way to break the ice, and suddenly the questions were coming from all corners of the room.

'When did it happen?'

'Was there much damage done?'

145

'What did they take?'

The last query seemed to be the most insistent, as it came from several people at once. Oddly enough, the barrage seemed to restore Roger's confidence, but after all he had been coming to Grunning's Hole for years and knew practically everybody in the village. 'They don't seem to have taken anything,' he said good-humouredly. 'At least, not so far as I can see.'

'Made a proper mess of the place, Mrs Carter said.'

'Well ... yes. But no real damage done.' He picked up the tankards which Simms had shoved across the counter to him, and began to thread his way back across the crowded room.

'A bit odd that, i'n't it?' said one of the men, more persistent than the others; but Roger was concentrating on reaching his table without spillage, and made no reply.

'We'll go as soon as we finish this,' he muttered to Antony as he sat down again.

'Oh, I don't know about that.'

'Why not?' Roger was frowning, his mood this evening uncharacteristically mercurial.

'It's comfortable here,' said Antony negligently. 'Besides, I'm interested in your neighbours.'

'Why on earth—?' He broke off as he met Antony's eye. 'You're reading too much into what happened,' he concluded.

'Perhaps I am.' The talk had become general again now, and there wasn't much chance of their being overheard. 'Saturday night,' he went on thoughtfully. 'Do you know most of the people here?'

Roger took his time looking around him. 'All of them,' he said at last.

'And would you say they were fairly representative of the village?'

'Nearly all the older ones are here. A few of the young ones will be playing darts in the public, I expect.'

'I see.'

He still sounded thoughtful, and Roger said rather impatiently, 'What are you expecting to happen?'

'I'm not *expecting* anything, just hoping. But if there are any more questions try not to be so—so repressive, will you?'

'If you say so.' Roger tasted his beer and evidently found it to his liking, for he drank deeply before going on. 'Making a mountain out of a molehill,' he said then. But he sounded resigned, and did not again make any mention of leaving.

So they were still there when closing time was called and the bar began to empty. Antony had kept his eyes and ears open, but nothing had been done or said that could possibly be construed as significant. Probably Roger was right, and his instinct was at fault in telling him that if Uncle Hubert *had* used Grunning's Hole as a hiding place somebody local must share the secret with him. Now he drank the last of his beer, which he had been preserving as an excuse to linger, and as he put down the mug again a little man in a blue seaman's jersey stopped by their table and asked,

'How's the old man?'

Roger looked up. 'The ... what old man?' he said after a moment.

'Why, him as used to come down here ... to visit you, he said, though I don't recall as he was ever here at the same time as what you was.' He was a thin wisp of a man, but his hands were large and Antony wouldn't have minded betting they had some strength in them. He wouldn't have minded betting either that this time there was some malice behind the question ... it might be from some particular dislike of Roger, or just a general love of making mischief. 'Don't remember his name. Denton ... Benton ... something like that. Heard he was staying with you.'

Roger had evidently taken his friend's admonition to heart. 'Denning,' he said now, as though the query were the most natural in the world. 'He's perfectly well.'

'That's good.' He would have left then, if Antony hadn't detained him with a gesture.

'Just a minute, Mr—'

'Lambert,' said the little man. 'Pleased to meet you. Any friend of Mr Farrell's—'

'Yes, I'm sure. What I wanted to ask you, Mr Lambert, is this: how did you know where Mr Denning is?' He added, as the other hesitated, his brows drawn together in a frown, '*That* wasn't in any newspaper, so far as I'm aware.'

'No, of course not.' Disconcertingly, Lambert tittered. 'It seems to me ... Bill told me. Didn't you, Bill?' he called across to the landlord, who paused in his task of polishing glasses to give him a blank look. 'Mr Farrell's friend here,' the little man explained, 'wants to know how you knew the old gentleman—Mr Farrell's uncle—is staying with him.'

'Oh, that!' Simms raised the glass he was holding and examined it critically against the light. 'Seems to me somebody told me that,' he said. He put down the glass and looked directly at Antony. 'Why would you want to know now?'

'Idle curiosity, I'm afraid.' His tone was casual. 'It isn't in the least important.'

In some contrary way, this seemed to act as a spur to Simms's memory. 'Now I comes to think of it,' he said slowly, 'seems it were Sam Fletcher told me. Is that right, Sam?'

Fletcher was the big man who had first addressed them that evening; he was still sitting in his corner by the fire, though his cronies had gone now and the room was almost clear. He finished his beer deliberately before he replied, 'Might 'a' been me,' with a shrug. 'Then again, it might not.'

'You knowed about it,' the landlord insisted. In some obscure way he seemed to feel that the honour of the house depended on being able to give the stranger in their midst a satisfactory answer to his question.

'I did,' Fletcher admitted. 'Now, who could have told me?' He got up and carried his empty mug across to the counter, apparently deep in thought, then he turned and met Maitland's eye with something of amusement in his own. 'Can't say I remembers, sir,' he added. 'Acourse, it might have been Dick Lambert, seeing as he knowed it too.'

'Not me,' said the little man firmly.

'It doesn't really matter,' Antony assured him. 'Come on, Roger, we may as well go and let Mr Simms finish clearing up.'

The evening had turned chilly, but the cool air was welcome after the fug in the bar. 'I hope you're satisfied,' said Roger, not too cordially, but when Antony only replied, 'A pleasant evening,' he took the hint and did not speak again until they were safely inside the cottage, and then not until the door was closed, the curtains drawn, and the lamp on the sideboard was once more shedding its warm light across the room. 'What was all that in aid of?' Roger asked then.

'Don't you think it's odd—to say the least of it—that somebody in the village knows where Uncle Hubert is?'

'Not particularly. Things do get about, you know they do.'

'I grant you they know where he's *been*. Seven years ago the case was widely reported. But can you see the social page of the local rag printing coyly, "Mr Hubert Denning has come out of prison and is staying with his godson in Beaton Street, Chelsea"?'

'When you put it like that,' said Roger slowly, 'I suppose it *is* rather odd.'

'Of course it is! Somebody has inside knowledge.'

'But how—?'

'You haven't been censoring Uncle Hubert's mail, have you? Well then!'

'You mean, someone down here helped him dispose of the gold?'

'It's a working hypothesis.'

'I don't see Uncle Hubert trusting anyone with a secret like that.'

'Yes, but that's where he was clever,' said Antony enthusiastically. 'If it's one of the villagers, he wouldn't know how to dispose of a single gold bar, let alone about a ton of the stuff.'

'A ton?' said Roger, bewildered.

'I'm speaking figuratively. I haven't really the remotest idea ... but that isn't important, Roger. If he has an accomplice here—'

'It could be anyone in the village,' said Roger, with the obvious intent of dampening his ardour.

'I daresay. All the same—'

'You're going to tell me it could have been one of those three men we talked to tonight.'

'Well, it could.'

'Not Lambert,' Roger objected. 'It seems pretty clear he heard it from Simms.'

'Who is Lambert, anyway?'

'The local butcher.'

'He doesn't look—'

'What the hell does that matter?'

'It doesn't, I suppose. Anyway, if I grant you Lambert's innocence it still leaves Simms and—what was the other chap's name?—as possibilities.'

'Fletcher. He's the sexton,' said Roger dryly.

Antony was unabashed. 'I like it,' he said, and grinned at his friend. 'I can just see Uncle Hubert coming out of evensong with his head full of nefarious schemes. Where does the fellow live?'

'When you go up the lane by the pub you come to, first, the vicarage, then the church, and then there's Fletcher's cottage.'

'Anything beyond it?'

'No, it's a dead end. But I don't see—'

'I like it,' said Antony again, but before Roger could respond the telephone rang, and he went out into the kitchen to answer it.

'I've been ringing and ringing,' said Jenny agitatedly when he lifted the receiver. From the other room Antony heard Roger's voice sharpen as he replied,

'What's up?'

'You'll have to come back straight away,' said Jenny. 'Only, do be careful, Roger. I mean, it's no good driving at ninety all the way and smashing yourselves up.'

'What is it, Jenny, what's the matter?'

'It's Meg, Roger. I hate to tell you. She disappeared from her dressing-room during the interval, and nobody knows where she is.'

## Sunday, 26th April

### I

It was obvious enough, even before Roger put down the receiver and came back into the living-room again, that something was seriously wrong. He told Antony what had happened in almost the same words that Jenny had used to him, and added only, 'I'll get the car out. Will you see to the lamps and make sure the doors are locked?' There was a blank look in his eyes which Antony misliked, and he spoke in response more sharply than he had intended, as though there was a need somehow to cut through a shell in which the other man had encased himself.

'Just a minute, Roger. Did Jenny give you any details?'

'Isn't the fact enough?'

'Yes, of course. I ... will you trust me, Roger, and not take it amiss if I say I'm staying here?'

That brought a momentary look of blank incomprehension; then Farrell shook his head as though to clear it. 'This idea of yours ... it won't do any good.'

'Let me try, at least. If you go to Uncle Nick ... Jenny will have done that already,' he corrected himself. 'He has more influence than I have at Scotland Yard.'

Roger made no attempt to argue. 'Yes, I'll do that.' He began to move towards the door, and then turned and said, as though the words were forced from his lips, 'Do you think ... Boney Nelson? What will he have done with her?'

No one knew better than Antony did of what small value reassurance was, when everything one cared about was in the balance. He said as steadily as he could, 'She'll be all right, if he means to use her as a hostage,' and hoped his

152

own stifling sense of panic was not evident in his tone.

'If that's what it is,' said Roger, with sudden violence, 'I shan't go near the police.'

'You—'

'Don't you see, Uncle Hubert's the only one who can help? If anyone communicates with you here, tell them I'll be at home and ready to co-operate. If I have to strangle the old boy myself—'

'Roger, for heaven's sake—'

But Roger did not even attempt to reply. The door opened, and closed behind him with a slam. A moment later Antony heard the roar of the Jensen's engine as he backed out into the road and drove off in the direction of the village. Antony waited until the sound had died away, then shrugged his shoulders slightly and went out to the telephone in the kitchen and dialled his own number. He wasn't sure where Jenny would be, but it seemed most likely...

And, sure enough, she answered on the first ring. 'Roger's on his way up to town,' he told her. 'I want—'

'Antony ... aren't you coming too?'

'Not immediately.'

'But I thought ... didn't he tell you what's happened?'

'Don't argue, love. Roger understands ... at least, I think he does. I want you to tell me exactly—'

'Yes, of course. Antony, you do realise, don't you? It's Meg!'

'I ... there's nothing I could do by coming home, Jenny.' There was a hint of desperation in his voice. 'Except, per-haps, to prevent Roger doing something foolish, and I think I can trust you and Uncle Nick to do that.'

'I see.' Her tone was subdued, and he was pretty sure she didn't understand in the least degree, though she would trust him blindly. 'Will he be coming here, Antony? Uncle Nick's here with me.'

'We'll talk about that in a minute. Tell me, love—'

'Yes, of course. I'm sorry.' She plunged into her explana-tion, speaking rather quickly, so that he thought, if Jenny has lost her serenity ... 'I went to the theatre,' she said, 'so that I could go home with Meg, and they found me a seat, not a very good one, and the detective who was with me had to stand at the back, I think. And the play was going along as usual—Meg's marvellous, you know, you'd never realise she was worried—until the interval, and even then of course I didn't realise anything was wrong straight away, but it just went on and on. And then someone came out and said that Miss Hamilton was "slightly indisposed", and her understudy would take over the part for the last act. So I just flew round to the stage door, and my detective with me, and everything behind the scenes was in the most frightful turmoil, and Meg wasn't there.'

'Had anybody—? No, I'm sorry I interrupted, love. Go on.'

'It's rather difficult to explain,' said Jenny. 'I don't know if you know the stage door of the *Cornmarket Theatre*, Antony; there's a little room where the door-keeper sits and keeps warm, and brews up tea, and Meg's policeman was with him.'

'Hadn't they seen anything suspicious? They must have—'

'Well, I suppose they had, Antony.' Her voice quivered dangerously, but she went on with a brave attempt at calmness, 'Only, you see, they were both dead ... shot.'

He thought he said, 'No!' but it was really more a groan than an exclamation.

Jenny said sympathetically, 'I know.' And then, after the barest pause, 'I've been terrified ever since I heard.' This time there was no doubt of the effort her self-control cost her. 'Do you think ... do you think Meg's dead too?'

'If it's any consolation to you, I think she's a hostage for our—and Uncle Hubert's—good behaviour. That's what I wanted to say to you, Jenny. Will you go round to Beaton Street right away, you and Uncle Nick? Roger will go straight there, unless I'm very much mistaken, and he didn't exactly take the news stoically.'

'You want us to stop him doing anything ... silly,' said Jenny, pausing over the word as though she was aware of its weakness. 'Antony, don't you think if Uncle Nick talked to Mr Denning—?'

'I was going to suggest it. At least, it can't do any harm. But I don't think—don't get your hopes up, love—I don't think he has the faintest feeling of responsibility for Meg or anyone else.'

'After she's been so good to him—'

'Don't count on it, that's all.' He paused, and then gave the conversation another twist. 'What happened after you got round to the stage door and encountered the police?'

'I made them call Inspector Sykes. I had to be quite fierce with them, Antony, but it seemed to me so very important. And then I telephoned Uncle Nick. We all of us finished up at Scotland Yard, which is why I was so long ringing you, though it didn't matter as it happened because you were still out somewhere when I first tried. And Superintendent Briggs was there, and I quite understand now why you dislike him so much. I think he's a horrible man.'

If he had been less worried that would have amused him, and even as it was he had a brief vision of Jenny, stiff with indignation, her grey eyes sparkling dangerously, confronting the portly detective. 'The important thing is,' he said, as though she knew all about this lapse into irrelevancy, 'what did he have to say?'

'I can hardly tell you, Antony, it made me so angry. He implied that Meg had disappeared with Roger's connivance, to place him in a good light, and to make the story *you* had told Inspector Sykes more credible. Of course, he didn't dare say anything too obvious against you with Uncle Nick there, it was all implications.'

'So the police aren't doing anything.'

'Well, of course they are, Antony, because of the two dead men. I mean, one of them was a policeman. And Inspector Sykes went with us to the lift when we left, and told us not to worry too much about Meg, so I'm sure he'll see that something is done about her as well.'

'Roger has an alibi, if that's any help. We were in the

pub with practically the entire male population of Grunning's Hole from dinner time on.'

'I don't think it will help really. Superintendent Briggs would just say he had a gang to—to carry out his orders.'

'Doesn't he believe in Boney Nelson's threats?'

'I think his attitude is that if two rival gangs wipe each other out that's all to the good.'

'Yes, I see. Will you let me talk to Uncle Nick for a minute, love? There are one or two things—'

But when he heard his uncle's voice, he didn't immediately know what to say. Sir Nicholas said heavily, 'This is a bad business, Antony.' And then, 'I gather you're still at Grunning's Hole, but surely—'

'Roger left as soon as we heard about Meg.'

'I take it then that you had some reason for remaining behind.'

'Yes, of course. It goes back to the fact that the cottage here was searched, Uncle Nick. I told you about that.'

'I have no doubt that set you guessing again.' Sir Nicholas sounded resigned.

'Well, it did. I think one of Hubert Denning's former employees has given Boney Nelson the idea that the gold may be hidden here, or hereabouts. And if that happens to be right, what is more likely than that the old boy has a local accomplice?'

'Have you any evidence to that effect?'

'N-no.'

'You must be able to answer that, one way or the other.'

'It all depends what you mean by evidence.' Sir Nicholas made a sound uncommonly like a snarl. 'Somebody here knew that Uncle Hubert was out of prison and staying with Roger, and spread the information about the village,' Antony explained. 'I don't know whether you'd call that evidence or not.'

'Nothing that the police would accept,' said Sir Nicholas slowly.

'I gather you had a rather abortive session at Scotland Yard.'

'Not altogether useless, I fancy. I tried to get in touch with Sir Edwin, of course—'

'The Assistant Commissioner?' Antony sounded startled, but then he added more slowly, 'Yes, I suppose you would do that.'

'You may give me credit for so much ingenuity. Unfortunately he was out, and the only result of my invoking his name at headquarters was to bring Chief Superintendent Briggs on the scene. But whatever he believes, or professes to believe, some action will be taken.'

'Yes, of course. Particularly as one of the dead men was a police officer. But I'm horribly worried about Meg, Uncle Nick.'

'So are we all.' But Antony didn't need telling that, he was used to Sir Nicholas's ways. 'I am still not clear what good you think you are doing, remaining in Grunning's Hole,' his uncle went on.

'You can take care of things in town, Uncle Nick. It doesn't seem likely that Boney Nelson will take her to any of his known hide-outs. But supposing he brings her down here.'

'Why should he do that?'

'To be on the spot when—when something snaps. He thinks both Roger and I know where the gold is, you know, and either of us would be ready enough to divulge the secret in return for Meg's safety.'

'Hm,' said Sir Nicholas. It was impossible to tell what he really thought of the suggestion. 'You're saying he may come to the cottage?'

'Where else?' He sounded more confident than he felt. 'Even if he knows, or guesses, that Roger and I came down here, he'd assume we both left for town as soon as we heard what had happened to Meg.'

'That sounds a little far-fetched, even for one of your ideas.'

'Like to bet on it?' He had never felt less like being flippant in his life, but at the same time he was conscious

of a cold fear that he was right, which at all costs he wished
to hide.

'I should not.' Sir Nicholas's tone was austere. 'But isn't
that rather a dangerous game, Antony ... waiting there for
him?'

'You pointed out yourself I'm most likely wrong in my
assessment of the situation. *If* I'm right, I can hardly leave
Meg to face him alone.'

'No, I see. Are you armed?'

'I didn't foresee the necessity when we came down here.
In any case, Nelson isn't likely to be alone. It wouldn't do
much good unless I shot the whole mob out of hand, and
before I could do that one of them would surely be quick-
witted enough to grab Meg and use her as a screen; and
after that—'

'Yes, I see your point; it is an academic one anyway. But
you must have some plan,' said Sir Nicholas irritably.

'Only to play it by ear. Well, I have a sort of idea,' Antony admitted. 'But it's rather vague, and it wouldn't do
any good to go into it now.'

'I've half a mind to come down there myself.'

'No! It's much more important to wait for Roger,' he
added hurriedly. 'Besides, if Boney Nelson *is* on his way
down here, you'd be too far behind him to do any good.'

'Is there a local constable?'

'His presence would invalidate my plan, you see ... such
as it is.' He sounded apologetic, and was relieved when his
uncle did not press the point.

'Then all I can do is to talk to Sykes again, if he's available. If I could give him any definite information—'

'Obviously you can't do that, Uncle Nick.'

'No ... precisely!' This was said with something of a
snap. 'What I can't understand,' Sir Nicholas added, after
a pause, during which his nephew sought in vain for something to say, 'is why your friend Mr Nelson should come
so far into the open. He must know he will be suspected
of tonight's outrage, yet he killed twice, apparently without a second thought ... and one of the men, as you have

reminded me, was a detective constable. I think there is no doubt—I don't think Jenny told you this—that he would have killed Meg's dresser as well if she hadn't been temporarily absent on some errand or other.'

'I've been thinking about that too,' said Antony. 'For one thing, he's got away with plenty already, from what Sykes told me; perhaps he sees himself as invincible. For another, it would prove he meant business'—his voice wasn't altogether steady as he said this—'prove how little chance Meg has unless we're willing to give him what he wants.'

'Even so—'

'There's one other thing, Uncle Nick. Something Sykes said made me wonder if perhaps they were getting a line on Nelson at last ... something they could prove against him, I mean. If that is so, and he has any idea of it at all, he may be desperate to make a killing and retire abroad. If the gold is really worth a million, it would certainly comfort him in his exile ... don't you think?'

'One argument contradicts another,' said Sir Nicholas coldly. 'I suppose you realise that.'

'I hadn't ... yes, I see what you mean. Anyway, for one reason or another—'

'I incline to the third possibility.' Sir Nicholas's voice faded and then came more strongly again, as though he had turned his head momentarily. 'If I am to follow your example, and indulge in the deplorable habit of conjecture, I should surmise that Roger intends to go immediately to his home.'

'Yes. I told Jenny—'

'Then I—or rather we—will repair there straight away.'

'There's no desperate hurry. He can't possibly be there for a couple of hours, even if he drives like the devil.'

'As no doubt he will. I can get in touch with you at the cottage, then, if necessary?'

'Better not. If Boney doesn't come I'll call you. And ... Uncle Nick ... don't let Jenny out of your sight.'

This time there was a pause before Sir Nicholas answered.

'I am not likely to do so,' he said at last, and replaced the receiver, very gently.

## II

Antony glanced at his watch after he had in his turn rung off, and indulged in a little mental arithmetic. If he was right—his mood was ambivalent, and he didn't know whether he hoped or feared it—Boney Nelson couldn't arrive here with his prisoner for at least another hour; that was, assuming he drove down at a reasonable pace, which he was pretty sure to do. In the circumstances, he wouldn't want to risk being stopped for speeding. But then, if he *did* come ... no use thinking of that, there was only one way of playing the hand that he could see, and if that failed circumstances would have to guide him.

Before he left the cottage he turned out the lamp, and damped down the fire that had been giving the room a semblance of comfort. Roger had gone off with the front door key in his pocket, but there was a spare one in the kitchen, he knew, so he fetched that and locked up carefully behind him. Not that he expected to be gone long...

It was a moonless night, but he could see well enough once he had allowed his eyes to adjust to the darkness. The tide was in, and as he walked towards the village he could hear the waves lapping against the jetty, and see dimly the outline of several small boats that rode at anchor out in the stream. Roger's *Windsong* would be among them, and he wondered for a moment whether he had been right in dismissing it from his calculations. But Boney Nelson would see as well as he did that it would have been an impossible hiding-place, nor would he have considered it for a moment as a place to bring Meg. The difficulties were obvious enough, including the lack of a telephone.

The turning to the church lay on this side of the *Cross Keys*. He remembered the building itself well enough, though he had only visited it once, the first time he came to the cottage. It was old, one at least of the arches being Norman, and parts of the foundation older still, though he couldn't speak to that of his own knowledge as the crypt wasn't open to visitors except by special arrangement. Roger said the age of the settlement should be obvious, without this added proof, because whoever Grunning had been he had clearly not come over with the Conqueror.

But though he remembered the church itself, he couldn't remember the lie of the land. The path led up steeply, a rough, stony surface on which it was difficult to walk quietly. There were fields on either side, also stony and infertile if memory served him; then came the vicarage, a vast, Victorian monstrosity, its windows darkened at this late hour; then the church, on the same side of the road, and finally, straddling the way and making a dead end of the lane, what must be the sexton's cottage. Light glimmered behind red curtains at one of the windows. Antony stood for a moment in the shadow of the churchyard wall, familiarising himself with the scene, and then turned back the way he had come. He couldn't see that the expedition had done the slightest good. He would like to have talked to Fletcher; if he was Uncle Hubert's accomplice it was possible that he would be more easily bluffed or terrorised than the old man. But until something was heard from Boney Nelson it wasn't safe to make a move in any direction. The reflection brought Meg into his mind again, and he swore quietly to himself as he went delicately down the path. Instinct had kept him here, but if he was wrong he had probably alienated Roger for good and all. While if he was right he felt himself, at best, a broken reed. If what he suspected was true, Boney Nelson could have the gold and welcome, in return for Meg's safety. There were two snags to that: one was how far he could trust a man who had proved himself over and over again a natural killer; and the other was that even if they came off safely there would still be the police suspicions to face when it became obvious that he had connived at Boney Nelson's escape.

But it was no use thinking of all that. One step at a time ...

The phone was ringing as he let himself into the cottage again. He found his way to it in the darkness and said 'Hallo' cautiously because he didn't quite know what to expect, but it was his uncle's voice that greeted him. 'We're in Beaton Street. Jenny and I arrived five minutes ago. I ventured to telephone because I think it is important that you should know ... there is no one in the house.'

For a moment the significance of that didn't register. He said foolishly, 'How did you get in then?' and remembered even as he spoke that Roger had given Jenny his key before they left for Grunning's Hole after lunch ... an eternity ago. He interrupted Sir Nicholas's rather testy explanation, saying urgently, 'Where's Uncle Hubert?'

'I have not the faintest idea.'

'The chap who was tailing him—'

'I have been the length of the street on both sides without discovering his body,' said Sir Nicholas precisely. 'Which inclines me to the belief that Mr Denning's disappearance was voluntary. I intend, however, to get in touch with the police again.'

'What a muddle! You haven't heard from Boney Nelson yet?'

'I don't expect to, until Roger has had time to get here.'

'No, of course. I won't keep you, Uncle Nick.' But after he had rung off he could think of a dozen questions he might have asked to delay the moment when his own solitariness would again be brought home to him.

He felt his way upstairs, still in the dark, and seated himself by the window of the front bedroom to await developments, and hoped, and feared, that they would come.


III


Meg's first feeling when she came to herself was one of confusion, which wasn't helped by the fact that her head was aching violently and that she felt a strong desire to be sick. She had identified the fact that she was in the back seat of a fast-moving car before she became aware of her own identity ... Meg Farrell, who was also Margaret Hamilton, and who should be on stage by now, coping with the complexities of the last act of *Five for a Farthing*. She puzzled over this for some moments, and it was only when she tried to put up a hand to push back an unruly strand of hair that she realised her wrists were tied and started to struggle, futilely, to release them. As she did so a voice beside her said reprovingly, 'That won't do you no good.'

She turned her head then, but couldn't see the man who had spoken clearly. The two men in the front seat were silhouettes, at least; a broad-shouldered fellow in front of her, and a shorter, slighter figure in the driver's seat. The cord was thin, and cruelly tight, so that it cut into her wrists even when she sat quite still; and she realised now that her ankles were bound too. 'Then you'd better untie me yourself, hadn't you?' she said imperiously, and thrust out her hands in a regal gesture, whose effect was unfortunately wasted in the darkness. But it was quite true that, just for the moment, she was more angry than fearful.

'I'm not likely to do that. Not yet,' the man in the corner said. Meg thought there was irony in his tone; but there was also, if she could have recognised it, a sort of unwilling respect.

'You've no right—'

'I've whatever rights I choose to take, my lady.' There was no doubt about the irony now. She forced her voice to reflect a coolness she did not feel.

'You must be Mr Nelson. Antony Maitland told me about you.' She was aware as she spoke that the echo of conventional politeness was absurd, but at the same time she could not bring herself to make use of his sobriquet.

'Boney Nelson, at your service,' he confirmed mockingly, so that Meg would have very much liked to slap him. As this was impractical she looked out of the window instead, and saw for the first time that they were running

163

through a darkened countryside. Somehow the fact that London was left behind seemed to make her plight more real to her, and she rounded again on her companion, saying hotly,

'How—?'

'You'll find there's nothing I don't dare,' said Boney Nelson complacently.

'I wasn't going to say that,' said Meg crossly. 'How did you manage to get me away from the theatre?'

'Don't you remember?' He sounded to be genuinely interested in her reply.

'I remember being in my dressing-room. That's all.' She had changed already for the last act, into the woollen dress of dusty rose colour, whose softness she could now feel under her hands. But after that...

'Well, Max hit you over the head before you could say anything,' said Boney Nelson prosaically, as though it was the most natural thing in the world, 'and I gave you a bit of an injection. Not much, just enough. You're not a very heavy weight, you know, and we met nobody on the way out to the car. If we had, it would have been just too bad for them.'

'But I don't understand. There was the door-keeper—'

'There was one of the fuzz, too. *They* won't bother no one no more.'

There was no mistaking his meaning. Meg said distressfully, 'Not old Soames!' But however much the old man's loss might grieve the theatre company, Soames had been alone in the world, whereas the policeman was young, and had a wife probably, and a family to mourn him.

'Did you have to do that?' she asked.

'They were in my way,' said Boney, with complete simplicity.

'It was awfully stupid of you,' said Meg spitefully. 'The police are bound to suspect you after what Mr Maitland has told them.' If she had stopped to think she would have realised that this wasn't the most sensible thing to say, but besides her sense of outrage, which she knew it would be useless to display, she was aware also of an almost over-whelming curiosity. Beneath both these emotions lay fear, which could no longer be denied, but she had no intention of letting her captor know it.

'*He* hasn't been near them,' said Boney Nelson confidently. 'Nor he won't ... now.'

'That's all you know,' Meg retorted, her dignity slipping a little. Boney Nelson chuckled; she thought that she had never heard so horrible a sound.

'Very close, him and your husband,' he said. 'And both of them'd be pleased to see you safe home again, I wouldn't wonder.'

'You're threatening me,' said Meg icily. The feeling of nausea was passing now, and though her head was throbbing the pain was not quite so acute as it had been in her first moments of consciousness. The man beside her laughed again.

'Did you think I was asking you to a party?' he asked. And then added, in a tone that was almost indulgent, 'If they'll play ball you'll be safe enough.'

'I'm not afraid of you,' said Meg, with all the fierceness at her disposal. And again, in reply, his voice was almost playful.

'Aren't you? That's because you don't know me very well.'

There didn't seem to be much to say to that, and a brief silence fell. In the darkness of her corner Meg was trying, gently this time, to see if there was any chance at all of loosening the cord about her wrists. It was a painful business, and she didn't think she was making any progress, but for all the care she took Boney Nelson must have been aware of movement.

He said, autocratically, 'Stop that!'

'It seems to me,' said Meg, her breath coming a little unevenly, 'that *you* must be afraid of *me*, Mr Nelson, if you need to keep me trussed up like this.'

He made no direct reply to that, but reached out and pulled her along the seat towards him, until she was half sitting, half lying within the circle of his arm. Meg struggled wildly, and tried to bring up both hands together to strike his face, but he only took them, together, into his own right hand, and held her with mortifying ease.

'If you don't keep still you'll hurt yourself,' he warned.

'Let me go!' panted Meg.

'Not just yet. Now isn't this more comfortable? No more flesh on your bones than what a sparrow'd have,' he added thoughtfully. 'But I like a bit of spirit myself.'

Meg was still now. She was conscious of his heart-beat, and of his breath upon her cheek. 'I hope you don't mean me to take that as a compliment,' she said.

'Why not? A chap like me could show you a bit of life.' His arm tightened about her waist, and he must have turned his head because his lips were very close to her ear when he added, 'What about it then?'

'Are you seriously suggesting—?' But she didn't try to finish the sentence. It was incredible ... it couldn't be happening ... but he *was* serious. 'I suppose,' said Meg viciously, abandoning whatever of dignity was left to her, 'this is the only way you can get your women ... by kidnapping them.'

She was frightened as soon as she had spoken. Her present position was humiliating and uncomfortable, but she didn't actually want to provoke him to violence, particularly because she realised now that any sort of skirmishing between them would only serve to excite him further. But in some odd way he seemed to take the words as a compliment, saying with another of his spine-chilling chuckles, 'That's it, my lady. No sport if you give in right away.'

'If you think—'

'I could tame you,' said Boney Nelson, not boasting, merely stating a fact. From somewhere Meg found the spirit to laugh in her turn.

'You're talking like a bad play,' she told him contemptuously.

'Am I then?' Again he seemed to find some obscure satisfaction in what she said. But as he spoke he released the grip which all this time he had kept on her hands, and when, encouraged by this, she again tried to wriggle herself free from his embrace, he did not attempt to stop her, and allowed her to push herself back into her corner again ... a surprisingly difficult business with wrists and ankles tied. But she managed it at last and leaned back, satisfied for the moment with so small a measure of freedom. As she did so she reflected for the first time on the odd fact that neither of the men in the front seat had shown the slightest interest in what was going on. Well, the driver couldn't turn round, of course, but she didn't think it was delicacy of feeling that kept the thick-set man staring stolidly ahead. Respect for his leader, perhaps; it seemed it was not only Boney Nelson's victims who needed to treat him with circumspection. She found no comfort in the thought, nor in the rather desolate look of the countryside that was flashing past the windows; it matched her mood. And Nelson's next remark, made in a tone which sounded like a rough attempt at consolation, only contributed to her wretchedness.

'Time for fun and games,' he said, 'after we've settled matters with that husband of yours.'

She considered for a moment before she answered that. She could say, 'How do you know he cares what happens to me?' but that might be regarded as encouragement, and she thought she would die if Nelson touched her again. She could repeat what Antony had already told him, that none of them knew where the gold was hidden, but there wasn't much chance he would believe her. And if he did, she realised for the first time, there wouldn't be anything to stop him killing her, or raping her, whichever best suited his mood. When he communicated with Roger and Antony, perhaps one of them could think of some way out. It wasn't much of a hope, but the best she could find. So she said instead, carefully, in a voice from which all emotion had been banished, 'Where are you taking me?'

'Where do you think?'

'How should I know?'

'Have a guess. Somewhere no one'll think of looking for us,' he added helpfully.

'Buckingham Palace,' said Meg. If the situation hadn't been so desperate she would have been amused when he took the remark at face value and answered seriously,

'Now, you can see for yourself we've left London.'

'Then to one of your—your hide-outs in the country, I suppose.'

'Wrong again.' For the moment he sounded almost jovial. 'Somewhere you know well, my lady ... somewhere you're fond of, or so I've heard.'

'Where then?'

'Grunning's Hole.'

'You must be mad!'

'Don't give me that.' The ugly note had crept into his voice again.

'But ... really, Mr Nelson!' She hoped that sounded conciliatory. 'It's a tiny place. How can you hide me there?'

'At your own cottage, where better? It's a tidy step from the village, and who's to know what goes on there?'

'But ... why?' she said helplessly.

'Three good reasons. I've told you one of them.' He seemed ready enough to talk; she thought his conceit must be overwhelming. 'It's the last place anyone'll think of looking for us—'

'But you'll have to tell Roger where we are,' Meg objected.

'Granted. But he's not likely to tell anybody else, except perhaps that lawyer pal of his.'

'I don't understand.' She wanted to keep his mind occupied, but she was also genuinely curious. 'You couldn't abduct me from the theatre without everybody knowing. The police as well.'

'Don't I know it! Fair foolish they'll look, won't they, having you picked up from under their noses?'

'Is that why—?'

'One reason.'

'But—'

'Don't worry about me,' he advised her kindly. 'You'll understand why it doesn't matter when I tell you why we're going to Grunning's Hole. Max—that's Max, sitting next to the driver—has a fair idea the old man hid the gold somewhere thereabouts; and when we've got our hands on it—and we shall get our hands on it by the time we've finished with you and your friends, my lady—we've got our escape route all lined up. A motor cruiser moored at Barton, about five miles further down the creek.'

It all sounded horribly specious. Meg was silent for a while, thinking it out; but she was afraid of silence now. It was a big car, but even with the width of the seat between them she was as conscious of his presence as she would have been of the ticking of an unexploded bomb. 'What— what are you going to do?' she asked, and for all her care her voice quavered a little as she put the question.

He answered it with another. 'What will your husband do when he knows what's happened?'

'I don't know.'

'What would anybody do when they knew a member of their family had been kidnapped?' Ridiculously, he sounded almost like a school-master; a school-master being patient with a not-too-bright pupil.

'Go home, I suppose,' said Meg slowly, 'and wait for a message.'

'That's right. He can tell me on the telephone, most likely, where the gold is hidden. If not—if he has to come down here and show us where it is—we can occupy the interval very comfortably, my lady, getting to know one another better.' He stretched out a hand again, to cover hers where they lay in her lap. 'What would you say to a trip to the continent?' he asked softly. 'All expenses paid.'

Meg quivered under his touch, and was still. The car rushed onwards through the darkness.

It was the car's headlights that alerted him, swinging wide
over the sea as it turned the corner, and then straight
along the lane to illumine only the banks and hedges on
either side. For a moment Antony thought it was going
past, then it slowed and turned into the gateway beside
the cottage at no more than a crawl. By the time it stopped
he could only see the glow of the rear lights, then these
too were extinguished and he waited, holding his breath, to
hear the car's doors open and then slam shut again. If it
was Boney Nelson he wasn't expecting the cottage to be
occupied, for at this late hour it could hardly be the darkened windows that reassured him. Or perhaps he just didn't
care.

The path came round too close to the front of the house
for him to see how many came from the car; he thought he
heard the footsteps of two men, and then after a short interval of a third, walking heavily and more slowly. They
weren't making any unnecessary noise now, but they weren't
being stealthy either. He got up and went quietly across
the room to stand at the head of the stair, where he could
look down and see the front door. There was a pause, a
scratching sound that could well have been a mouse in the
wainscot, then the door swung open and he had a momentary glimpse of shadowy figures on the threshold before an
electric torch swung its beam around the room. Then the
man who held it gave a grunt of satisfaction and made for
the lamp on the sideboard. He must have had matches in
his pocket, because there was only the briefest pause before he had it burning, but even as the light flickered he
said in a startled tone,

'The glass is still warm.'

'Then perhaps we're expected.' Antony recognised
Boney Nelson's voice before he saw him, the third man to
come into the room, with Meg in his arms. He carried her
easily across the room, and dumped her unceremoniously

in one of the chairs near the fireplace. When he turned his gun was out, and Antony saw that the other two men were similarly armed. He had time to notice only that Meg was bound, and to recognise in himself an unwelcome thrill of anger at the sight, before Nelson spoke again.

'Have a look round and see who's here ... if anybody.'

To give way to anger would be to cloud his judgment, would be, in consequence, a sort of betrayal. Antony said, 'No n-need to do that, I'm alone,' and began to come slowly down the worn stone staircase. Three guns were trained on him at once, but it wouldn't do either to show his fear. And he was afraid; Boney Nelson was about as dangerous as a hungry tiger, and a good deal more unpredictable. Maitland looked past him and said, as lightly as he could, 'Hallo, Meg.'

Meg said, 'Darling!' with something more heartfelt than usual in her tone. She was dressed for the final act, and even in the lamplight her make-up looked garish; her hair was dishevelled, her dress crumpled, and both her stockings were laddered, but there was a glint in her eye that told Antony she was very far from defeated. He gave her a smile that was meant to be encouraging, and turned his attention back to her captor.

Boney Nelson was giving him a hard stare, and his eyes did not move as he ordered his henchmen, 'Have a look round.'

'I don't,' said Maitland, 'like to see this lack of trust.' Nelson ignored the remark, and the other two men departed obediently, one through the door into the kitchen, the other up the stairs. There was an uneasy silence until they returned, each with a negative report, when Nelson said, as curtly as before,

'Search him.'

This, too, was accomplished in silence. Antony thought it was the small man who came up behind him, his hands were quick and deft; but with the other man somewhere in the background and Boney Nelson watching him like a hawk, there wasn't a chance of making a move.

'Nothing there,' the searcher reported at last.

'All right then. You'd better sit down, Maitland. Over there.' The chair he indicated was the twin to the one Meg occupied; deep enough to make any sudden movement difficult, if not impossible.

'I'd rather—'

'Or we can tie your hands. I thought,' said Boney Nelson, 'you might find that rather painful. Got a bad arm, haven't you? Or so I heard.'

Antony's lips tightened. He was tired, and his shoulder was hurting abominably, but he didn't want to think of that. 'That's . . . considerate of you,' he said carefully, after a moment. 'I was going to ask you to let me untie the cord round Mrs Farrell's wrists.'

'She stays as she is. Sit down!' said Nelson. 'I shan't tell you again.' He waited until Maitland had obeyed him and then asked abruptly, 'Where's Farrell, if he isn't here?'

'He left for London as soon as he heard what had happened. If you want to telephone him,' he added hopefully, 'I expect he'll be home by now.'

'Who let him know?'

'My wife.'

Nelson took time to think that out, and Antony was glad to see he found it reassuring. It was too much to expect, of course, that he would actually put through a call to Beaton Street from the cottage, but even so he felt a pang of disappointment when Boney shook his head decisively and said, 'But you stayed behind when he left. Why did you do that?' The question came sharply, but it was obvious that he was pleased with his own cleverness.

'I guessed you might come here,' said Antony, and saw the other man frown.

'That doesn't explain—'

'I should have thought it was obvious. You want to do a deal, don't you? It saves trouble, my being here.'

'Singing a different tune now, aren't you?' said Nelson, self-satisfied again.

'You made a proposition to me once.'

'That's out. I hold all the trump cards now.' He moved a little, so that he could rest his hand on Meg's shoulder, a proprietary gesture; but for all that he did not relax his vigilance in the slightest degree. Antony's anger, which he thought he had suppressed successfully, flared again.

'Tell me, M-meg, have they h-hurt you?'

'They hit me over the head, and then drugged me, and I've got a headache. Apart from that—' She was as aware as he of the danger of his losing his temper, and her tartness was as good as a tonic to him. He looked back at Nelson again and asked, almost casually,

'If I keep my part of the bargain, what then?'

'Don't trust him, Antony.' It was Meg who was frowning now, and he answered her without taking his eyes from Boney's face.

'I don't seem to have much choice.'

'But you don't *know*—'

'I can guess.'

'I want more than that,' said Boney Nelson roughly.

'It seems like an impasse, doesn't it?' said Antony cheerfully. 'I've already complained of your lack of trust.'

'Come off it! What are you offering?'

'To tell you where I think the gold is hidden. In return for Meg's safety, and my own.'

'Not good enough. If I buy at all I'm buying a certainty, not a random guess.'

'Then I've nothing to offer you. What do you suggest as an alternative?'

'Perhaps your friend Farrell may be more amenable.' As he spoke Nelson's hand tightened painfully on Meg's shoulder, too tightly for her to be able to squirm away from him.

'Why don't you call him then?' said Maitland, trying to ignore what he saw was happening. But that was a mistake, his tone was too eager. Boney looked at him frowningly.

'Want me to do that, don't you?' he said.

'Not particularly.'

'That's just as well. I know a trick worth two of that. When I'm good and ready Bill will take the car ... but

173

that may not be necessary, so long as you're here.'

'At least,' said Antony, making a good enough job of hiding his disappointment, 'it can't do any harm for you to hear what I've got to say. If you don't find the gold we're back in square one.'

The other man took time to look at this from all angles. Then he patted Meg's shoulder again. 'Sweet on her yourself, are you?' he asked. 'Mind you, it won't do her any good, or you, unless you tell me the truth.'

'The best I can do is . . . well . . . an educated guess.'

'Do you have to talk so fancy?'

'I was only trying to explain . . . but that doesn't matter. First, will you confirm one thing for me? You or some of your men searched this cottage, didn't you, because you had some reason to think that the gold might be hidden hereabouts?'

'There was three of us did it.'

'And you got the idea from something one of Hubert Denning's former associates told you?'

'That's right. Max and Bill, they both thought that.'

'If the gold is actually hidden in Grunning's Hole it seems likely that Denning had a local accomplice . . . don't you think?'

'What if he had?'

'There's another point,' said Maitland, ignoring the question. And went on, in almost the same words he had used to Sir Nicholas, 'Somebody here knew that Denning was out of prison and where he was staying. The information is all over the village, and I don't see where it could have come from except Denning himself.'

'Even if that's right, it doesn't help us.'

'It leads us a step further. There are two men who seem to be the most likely to have started the gossip. One is the landlord of the *Cross Keys*, and I suppose you could hide gold in a public inn, but it wouldn't be easy. The other is the sexton, a man called Fletcher, and if you can think of anyone with a better opportunity—' But he broke off there, when there was a soft tapping on the front door. At a sign from Nelson the smaller of his two associates went across to open it, gun in hand; and when he had pulled it open there was Hubert Denning on the doorstep, benevolent as ever but cautious, with his hands raised slightly above his head.

He looked all round the room before he spoke, taking in every detail, and perhaps it was a tribute to the force of his personality that nobody spoke while he did so. And then, 'I've been listening to you for several minutes, I'm afraid,' he said. 'I hope you won't consider it an unpardonable liberty. I always did admire your ingenuity, Mr Maitland.'

By this time Boney Nelson had recovered from his first surprise. He looked from Maitland to Denning, and back again. 'What in hell's name is going on?' he demanded.

'You haven't met Mr Denning?' said Antony. He hadn't worked out yet what difference this might make to his position, and Meg's, and frankly he feared the worst; but even so a slight hint of amusement crept into his voice, because there was something ridiculous, under the circumstances, about making a solemn introduction. 'Uncle Hubert—I hope you won't mind my calling you that—this is Boney Nelson.'

'Ah! The very person I wanted to see. You'll forgive me for suggesting it, Mr Nelson, but if one of these gentlemen were to search me—it's nice to see you again Max, and you, Bill—I could lower my arms from this rather uncomfortable position.'

Boney Nelson nodded curtly. It wouldn't last, of course, but for the moment he seemed fascinated by the newcomer. When Bill stepped back empty-handed a moment later Hubert Denning lowered his hands without asking for further permission, said casually, 'If you would be good enough to shut the door, Bill, the night air is chilly,' and came across the room until he stood behind the sofa that was opposite the fireplace. 'I am rather surprised to find so many of you here,' he remarked. 'Perhaps one of you will enlighten me as to what has been happening.' Raised eyebrows emphasised the mild enquiry.

'It's why you're here that wants explaining,' said Nelson. His voice sounded even rougher than usual by contrast with the old man's smoothness.

'I admit I did not expect ... but I am delighted to find you here, my dear fellow. I came down to see an employee of mine, to satisfy myself that all was well here; then when I came back to town I had intended to get in touch with you.'

'How did you get here?' For the moment it did not seem to Antony that there was anything to be done but swim with the tide, but he didn't see why his curiosity shouldn't be satisfied.

'By car, of course. When I had shaken off that tiresome policeman I merely went to one of the rental agencies. Did you really think that driving myself would be beyond me, Mr Maitland?'

'But when you got here, how did you know——?'

'I heard a car come through the village, late enough to need some explanation. So I took a stroll in this direction, saw the car parked outside—not Roger's car, which I would have expected to see there—and came up quietly to the door. Now I understand why Mr Nelson is here, and his associates, and as I said I'm pleased to see them. But you, Meg? You and Mr Maitland. I hope you haven't been playing fast and loose with Roger's affections.'

Meg appeared for the moment incapable of speech, which wasn't like her. Boney, making a recovery, said bluntly, 'I brought her here.'

'Against her will, I perceive. You grieve me, my dear sir, you do indeed. Then Mr Maitland is here merely in the role of a knight errant, and not a very successful one, as far as I can see.'

'Not successful at all,' Antony agreed. 'The floor is all yours, Mr Denning. Perhaps you'll have better fortune.'

'I came here to make a proposition to Mr Nelson, certainly. It concerns nobody but the two of us.'

'If you can persuade him to let Meg go——'

'Why should I? Her safety is Roger's concern, though

176

he is not here, and you seem to have made it yours. It is none of mine.'

'Do you m-mean to s-stand there—?'

Boney Nelson had had enough of this exchange. He said, 'Quiet!' in a tone that somehow Antony didn't feel like disregarding. And then, to Denning, 'What's all this about a deal?'

'Mr Maitland informed me the other evening that you had offered a sum of £90,000 in all for information as to the whereabouts of the gold which I have hidden away. As neither he nor Roger is interested in taking you up on this it occurred to me that perhaps we could do business together.'

'Why should you now be willing—?'

'The loss of Stoker's help has created difficulties for me. I need assistance in moving the gold. Besides, I am an old man and my needs are few. £100,000, for instance, is a nice, round sum.'

'Why should I give you anything? Maitland's already said he's ready to do a deal.'

'For two reasons. He may be able to guess vaguely the location of the gold, but not its precise location. More importantly, he cannot give you the help that I can give you in disposing of the bullion abroad.'

'Now you're talking!'

'I am relieved to hear you say so. Is it—er—is it a deal then?'

'It's a deal!' All this time his eyes had been fixed coldly on Maitland's face, but now, though the gun remained steady, there was no mistaking the jubilation in his look. 'Start talking,' he said.

'Before I do will you indulge me by allowing me to hear what Mr Maitland was about to say when I came in?'

'Why should you want—?'

'A matter of interest, my dear fellow, a matter of interest.'

Antony said, slurring the words a little as if he were nervous, 'Go to hell!' He had hoped—it was all he could hope —that while the search for the gold was going on he would have some opportunity for action, but now that Uncle Hubert had taken a hand in the game ...

The old man looked pained. Boney Nelson let go of Meg's shoulder and grabbed instead a handful of her hair, jerking her head back so that she cried out with the pain of it before she shut her lips tightly against the sound. Antony said, 'Stop that!' and put his hands on the arms of his chair to pull himself up, but before he could do so Max came up behind him and pulled him back with an ungentle hand, jarring his shoulder. He met, at the same time, a look from Nelson that was coldly malignant.

'So ... talk,' Boney commanded.

'Take your hands off her then.'

Boney shrugged, but that seemed to be his way of agreeing. He released his grip on Meg's hair and her body, which had stiffened, relaxed against the cushion. She didn't say anything, but Antony met her eye and was angry again ... angrier even than he had been before. He stumbled a little over his first words, and thought that perhaps it would be a good thing if they believed him in the grip of panic. He had tricked Uncle Hubert once, seven years ago; it wasn't possible, surely, that he could do so again. And Boney Nelson ... what sort of a judge was he of men?

'I w-was g-going to s-say,' said Maitland, 'that if I w-was looking for a cache I'd think of the church first of all ... if I had access to it, that is. And then ... the crypt perhaps? I don't *know*.'

'How very gratifying it is,' said Uncle Hubert benignly, 'to realise that I didn't underrate you.'

'Am I right?' He gave a quick, nervous laugh. 'You didn't need Denning after all, you see,' he said to Nelson.

'You're forgetting his connections abroad,' said Boney. He too sounded almost amiable now.

'That's just what I mean,' said Antony earnestly. 'Who's to say you won't wake up one morning with your throat cut?'

'Really, Mr Maitland!' Hubert Denning protested.

'I wouldn't trust him an inch if I were you. Not an inch,' said Antony, ignoring him.

'Don't worry about me.' Boney was confident. 'I can take care of myself.'

Uncle Hubert, however, was not quite at ease. 'You could ask Max and Bill for their opinion of my trustworthiness,' he suggested. 'They know me, after all.'

'Yes, Max and Bill,' said Maitland, screwing his head round until he could see Bill, but not Max who was still standing behind his chair. He wished Meg wasn't watching him so intently, his eyes were drawn towards hers and he needed to concentrate, and he couldn't bear the pinched look on her face, which reminded him only too vividly of a time he would rather forget. 'You're in on this deal, I suppose, but how many of your colleagues are being left out of it? Can you really trust Boney Nelson, do you think?'

'That's enough!' That was Uncle Hubert, himself again, and Antony felt his hackles rising at the dictatorial tone.

'There's a chap in London you've promised a cut to as well,' he said, with what he felt was a nicely judged air of desperation. 'Whoever stole Meg's key and gave it to you. Or are you going to double-cross him as well?'

'There'll be no double-crossing.' Nelson's tone was oddly equable. 'You know so much,' he said mockingly. 'Do you know who he is too?'

'I think I do.'

'Who then?' He was obviously incredulous, but it was not this that prompted Maitland's reply; Boney was still standing near Meg, and could hurt her again in an instant.

'Farrell's partner, Sam Reade,' said Antony.

'How d'you make that out?'

'It's a long story. Am I right?'

'You are. Not that the knowledge is going to do you a bit of good, you know,' he added, shaking his head. 'But it's a pity, all things considered, that you didn't see your way to coming in with us when I asked you.'

'I believe that's a compliment,' said Antony, surprised.

'Near enough to one, anyway. Not that I don't like a chap with a bit more nerve.' He turned his head then, almost for the first time, to look squarely at Uncle Hubert. 'Are you prepared to show us . . . now?'

'Certainly I am. May I ask what your plans are then?'

'To leave the country immediately.'

'Very good. Each bar of gold, I should tell you, weighs one thousand troy ounces, or seventy pounds if you prefer to put it that way, so it should not be beyond your capabilities, particularly as you can use the car I have parked by the churchyard gate—'

'How many bars?'

'Again, seventy.'

'Any digging to do?'

'No, it is quite easily accessible.'

Boney was doing sums in his head. 'We should move that easy by daylight,' he said. He was businesslike now. 'Get up, Maitland. One of you, tie his hands.'

For a change, Hubert Denning spoke with something like agitation. 'I should recommend, I really should recommend, my dear fellow, that you dispose of your prisoners before we go to the church. Mr Maitland . . . it really would not be safe—'

'What can he do if we tie him up?' Boney sounded contemptuous, and the old man answered more slowly, and with great emphasis,

'I do assure you, it would be most unwise to underestimate him. He changed his tone quickly enough, if you noticed, when you touched Mrs Farrell.'

'He stays alive till I know if I want him,' said Nelson flatly. (So perhaps the pin-pricks, the talk of double-crossing, hadn't been altogether wasted.) 'As for the girl . . . we'll see.'

'Then I implore you, take Mr Maitland with us, so that you can keep an eye on him. I do assure you,' he said again, 'it isn't safe to leave him alone.'

Boney Nelson sighed, but then he shrugged his shoulders. 'As you like,' he said. 'Tie his hands, Max—behind his back, you fool—and gag the girl. And find a chair you can tie her to, there's probably one in the kitchen. No use taking any chances.'

## V

The night was cold, as Uncle Hubert had intimated, but that was just one more discomfort, and not the worst of them. Max's hands had not been gentle. Thin cord cut into Maitland's wrists, and in the tying of it his shoulder had been wrenched unmercifully, so that instead of the usual dull ache it now felt very much as if it were on fire. No time to think of that; no time to think of Meg, alone and—he was sure for all her stoicism—frightened. There had been something queer in Boney Nelson's attitude to her, something he disliked without being able to define it, but there was no time for that either; or to think of Jenny, and Roger, and Uncle Nick, who couldn't be very happy as they waited for news; or to wish that Hubert Denning hadn't interfered and that he had been left in the cottage, as Nelson had at first intended, because surely then he could have devised something...

But things were as they were. Uncle Hubert marching ahead, erect and spry as a two year old; himself next in line, with the other three ranged somewhere behind him. He wouldn't answer for Max and Bill, but he was uneasily conscious of Boney's attention malevolently concentrated on seeing that he didn't make a single false move. He was alert, as experience had taught him, for any opportunity; but he had to fight a growing conviction that none would come his way.

Along the lane ... the village was quiet still, sunk in slumber; up the stony track to the church. Uncle Hubert paused by the lych-gate, where a car was already parked, and spoke in a whisper. 'I'll get Fletcher. He has the key, and a couple of hurricane lanterns which it will be quite safe to use in the crypt. The door is on the other side, if you want to go there and wait for me. Not overlooked by the vicarage.'

He disappeared into the darkness. Boney Nelson said, 'Forward,' and Antony began to make his way unwillingly up the uneven, overgrown path that led round the church. There was the door that must be the one they needed, six steps down and the earth cut away on either side ... heavy oak and heavy iron hinges, and a keyhole that looked about big enough to drive a bus through.

Sure enough the key, when it came, was a big one; in Fletcher's hands it turned easily and silently. The man still had his air of secret amusement; he showed no surprise at seeing Antony again, and it seemed that whatever arrangement he had come to with Hubert Denning was satisfactory to him. He went in ahead of them, and did not turn up the wick of the storm lantern he carried until he was well inside; the old man went behind him with the second lantern, and the others followed in the same order as before.

In the flickering light it was an eerie place, and the smell of damp and decay didn't make it any more welcoming. Boney Nelson was breathing heavily now, his usual pose of being unmoved by events shattered in the excitement of coming near to his goal. Uncle Hubert raised his lantern and spoke like a showman.

'The last resting place of the Challis family, who were lords-of-the-manor hereabouts until they died out in 1736. The crypt hasn't been used since then.' As the light darted from one corner to another they could see four stone coffins, ranged together along the farther wall. 'The rest of them are underground,' he went on. 'The inscriptions are interesting, if you care for that sort of thing, but we shall not need to disturb them.'

'Get on with it,' Nelson growled. 'We've got no time to waste on this foolishness.'

'To business then.' The old man's cheerfulness was unimpaired. 'Max, and you Bill, if you will be good enough to give Fletcher a hand in removing the lid of the nearest coffin. It belonged to Roderick Challis, who died in the seventeenth century—the stone is too worn to make out the precise date—but you need not be afraid that you will find in it any grisly remains. He is—er—doubling up with an earlier Challis; not even cramped quarters, but in any case neither of them was in a position to complain.'

Fletcher put down his lantern on the second coffin, and the other two men pocketed their weapons and moved forward to help him with the heavy lid. Boney gestured with the gun he was still holding, implementing the gesture with the curt command, 'Over there!' and Maitland moved into the farthest corner of the crypt, turning so that he could lean against the sarcophagus that stood there and watch the men at work. But all the while he was conscious of Boney Nelson, standing a few paces away from him and no less vigilant than before. Uncle Hubert shifted his position a little and raised his lantern, so that the three men could see what they were doing.

By the time the lid was lifted and had thudded to the ground Bill, at least, was out of breath. Maitland was braced for action if Nelson moved his head, but Boney remained watchful, and only heaved a sigh of deep-felt satisfaction when Max announced jubilantly, 'It's there ... bars and bars of it.'

'All in the one coffin?'

'There was room for all of it and more,' Uncle Hubert assured him.

'Then get moving. You and Bill had better start off, Max, and Fletcher will give you a hand when one of you gets tired.'

It was a slow job, accompanied by a good deal of heaving and panting on the part of the men who were carrying it out. Antony lounged against the coffin and tried to decide when he should make his move. When Max and Bill—and their weapons—were outside together would be best, especially if they were still encumbered with one of the gold bars. He could tackle Boney Nelson, but there seemed no chance at all of taking him by surprise; and though he knew the attempt must be made sooner or later he grew less hopeful moment by moment that it would succeed.

He had lost count of the number of bars that had been moved, probably about twenty, when the faintest, most unexpected sound met his ears. Somebody moving cautiously outside, if he wasn't mistaken, moving stealthily down the stone steps to the open door. Hubert Denning still held his lantern high, his attention concentrated on Max and Bill who were delving together into the coffin for their next burden; Fletcher, too, seemed to hear nothing; and Boney Nelson—damn the man, would nothing distract him?—was as watchful as ever. Antony had time to wonder whether this might be the vicar, roused from his virtuous slumbers, and to hope it wasn't or the massacre that night was likely to be a wholesale one, when unbelievably in the doorway loomed the figure of a uniformed constable, whom he recognised more by his shape than by his features as P.C. Mason; and beside him a shorter, squarer man in tweeds levelling a double-barrelled shot-gun with both hammers cocked as if he knew how to use it.

And, at last, Boney Nelson's attention wavered.

As it did, three things happened at once. The tweedy man said gruffly, 'Hold it everybody'; Constable Mason—or so Antony swore later—said clearly, 'In the name of the law'; and Maitland, casual no longer, launched himself at Nelson, catching him with his shoulder somewhere about the midriff. Almost simultaneously, the gun went off.

For a moment all that Antony was conscious of was the pain in his shoulder, but when he picked himself up from the floor, sick and shaken, he found that the situation had crystallised a little. Boney Nelson was still on the floor, and seemed to be finding difficulty in getting his breath; he had let go of the gun and it had skidded almost to the constable's feet. Max and Bill had dropped the gold bar they had been wrestling with and, along with the sexton, had raised their hands ... he didn't blame them, the shot-gun had an ugly look. And Uncle Hubert had let fall his lantern, which flared up briefly and then went out; but even in the one remaining light it could be seen that he had a hole in his forehead from which the blood oozed sluggishly.

There was nothing to be done about it. When they got round to examining him he was very, very dead.

## VI

'No, of course I didn't intend it,' said Antony for the fifth time. 'It was a fluke that the shot hit him, but I still say it's better that way.'

'Well, I think it was very clever of you, darling,' said Meg, with her soul in her eyes. Roger made a face at her that probably meant, 'Don't tease him,' but Antony, who had been looking harassed, relaxed suddenly, and laughed.

'What I can't get over is the opportune arrival of Constable Mason,' he said.

Five people were sitting over a late tea in the Maitlands' living-room in Kempenfeldt Square; or perhaps it might better have been called breakfast. They had none of them got to bed before ten o'clock that morning—the Farrells using the spare room again because Jenny could hardly bear to let Meg out of her sight—and they had only just surfaced again. Only Sir Nicholas was heavy-eyed, because in spite of being up all night he had felt in honour bound to report on events in person to the Assistant Commissioner (Crime), whose name he had invoked so freely the night before. Antony was inclined to be wary of the apparent amiability of his mood, but the others were so pleased with themselves that they took it for granted. Boney Nelson's goose seemed to be very thoroughly cooked ... even in this enlightened age, kidnapping is a serious charge and murder an even more serious one; and even if it wasn't possible to prove the ownership of the gold—Sir Nicholas had his doubts, though the police apparently foresaw no difficulty—there was no doubt at all that he had no right to it.

'That,' said Sir Nicholas now, replying to his nephew, 'was due to Chief Inspector Sykes's intervention. I admit I was alarmed when he told me he would get in touch with the local constable, as well as with the district Detective Inspector, because the latter couldn't possibly be in time to do any good if you turned out to be right in your surmises, but he assured me the man could be relied on to behave with discretion.'

'Which he did,' said Antony, with a reminiscent grin.

'Yes, but I don't understand,' said Meg, 'how he came to have that angelic game-keeper with him.'

'You ought to. You heard it all explained.'

'I expect,' said Meg, with dignity, 'I was overwrought.'

'Well, I don't understand it either,' said Jenny. 'I heard Uncle Nick talking to Inspector Sykes, of course, but I thought it was too late to do anything because he couldn't get hold of him straight away.'

'For that matter,' said Antony, 'I don't know how you persuaded him to act on a hunch.'

'That, my dear boy, is simply explained. He thought you had some inside information, that you *knew* where Boney Nelson would make for.'

'I ... see.' Antony was thoughtful, but Roger interrupted his reverie.

'How did the game-keeper come into it? I don't understand that either.'

'He's a crony of Mason's, an old Provost Corps man, which forms a bond of sympathy between them. So I suppose it was natural that Mason should appeal to him for help. I admit, I've never been so glad to see anybody. Actually, the district people arrived half an hour later, which in a sense would have been in time.'

'If you hadn't done anything foolish in the meanwhile,' said Sir Nicholas.

'That, of course. Anyway, I think if they'd been first on the scene it would have resulted in a shoot out ... and where that would have led, goodness knows.'

There was a silence after that. Roger was the first to speak again. 'I'm grateful for the way things turned out, of course,' he said, giving Antony a grave look, 'and for what you did for Meg. But why didn't you tell me? Why did you let me come back to London?'

'Hasn't it occurred to you'—Maitland was glad of the chance to explain—'what the police would have thought if they'd found you in Boney Nelson's company somewhere in the vicinity of the gold? As it was, it was pretty obvious that Meg and I were telling the truth, but if you'd been there I bet we'd have found it considerably more difficult to convince the authorities that we were nothing but in-nocent bystanders.'

'If he'd been tied up, as you were, they wouldn't have thought he was in league with Boney Nelson,' Jenny objec-ted.

'No, but they'd have been of the opinion that you shared a guilty knowledge of the gold's whereabouts with Uncle Hubert, which you were prepared to barter for Meg's safety. I don't think they could have proved anything, mind, but on the whole it's better not to acquire a reputation like that.'

'I hadn't thought of that,' said Roger slowly.

'Don't think of it now,' Meg commanded him, and after a moment's hesitation he smiled at her. 'And I don't care what you think, darling,' she added ruthlessly, 'it's a good thing Uncle Hubert's dead, because now you don't have to worry what kind of mayhem he may cause in the future.'

'There is that, of course.'

'What I would like to know,' said Meg, 'what I could hardly get to sleep for wondering—'

'Liar,' said Roger, 'you slept like a log.'

'—is whether you were right, Antony, and Boney Nelson and Uncle Hubert would really have double-crossed each other if they got the chance.'

'I'd be willing to bet on it. Uncle Hubert, at least, was up to no good when he proposed a merger.'

'The other thing I'm puzzled about,' said Jenny, holding out her hand to take Sir Nicholas's cup for a refill, 'is why Uncle Hubert wanted to stay with Roger and Meg in the first place.'

'I haven't the faintest idea,' said Antony, after a moment's reflection.

Sir Nicholas took back his cup and put it down carefully. 'I should have thought that was the one thing that was obvious about this whole wretched business,' he said.

'Obvious?' echoed Antony, frowning.

'I think that Mr Denning had a better appreciation than you had of what the police attitude towards Roger was likely to be. He wanted to confuse and distract them, and you must admit he succeeded admirably in that.'

'So he did.'

'That ought to have been clear to you from the beginning,' said Sir Nicholas, gently malicious.

'Then let's talk about something else and forget all this,' said Jenny. Antony gave her a quick look, because that was one thing they could none of them do and she knew it; but then he saw her smile and thought that perhaps, after all, she had strength enough for the lot of them. At any rate, there was still something he had to say.

'About your key, Meg,' he began.

'Oh, yes, the key. Did you mean what you said to Boney Nelson, darling?'

'About Sam Reade,' said Antony. 'Yes, I did.'

'Sam Reade!' said Roger, much too loudly, 'I don't see why he should—'

'Do you see any reason for any of the others doing such a thing?'

'No, but that isn't to say ... I've always trusted him,' said Roger, as though that settled the matter.

Antony hesitated, and Meg said quietly into the silence, 'Boney Nelson confirmed it, darling.'

'But *why*? And what are you going to do about it?'

'We worked it out once, didn't we, that probably Boney Nelson got in touch with somebody he thought could help him get hold of a key? He may even be a client of Reade's, and know him that way. I expect you could find that out, Roger, if you set your mind to it.'

'Why didn't you suggest that before?'

'Because it never occurred to me. But to get back to Nelson, he might use bribery, he might use intimidation. Either would be an effective weapon, but most likely it was a mixture of both.'

'I see,' said Roger dully. And then, again, 'What are you going to do about it?'

'Nothing. Even if I told the police, and they believed me, there's nothing like proof.'

Sir Nicholas coughed, and they all looked at him expectantly. 'I have to agree with you about that,' he said. 'But —if you're sure of what you say, Antony—that isn't to say that Roger should take no action.'

'Boney Nelson confirmed it,' said Antony, as Meg had done, but now he was watching his friend. 'I don't see why he should have been lying about that.'

'He wasn't,' said Meg positively. 'But what I should like to know, darling, is how you knew.'

'A lot of little things,' said Antony. 'I think the main thing was David Reade's attitude. He could hardly have been so disingenuous as to believe that his own family and Terry's were automatically exempt from suspicion, but he always talked as if he assumed they were, which to me argued a guilty conscience. He himself could have obtained the key from Terry, but it didn't seem likely that Boney Nelson would have trusted anyone so young, and who in any case was only in touch with Roger at second hand, as it were. So it seemed likely that the guilty feeling was on his father's behalf.'

'You mean, he knew—?'

'Nothing so definite as that, but something must have made him suspicious.'

'It could have been because he thought Victor Barham—'

'No. That was ruled out by my talk with him. He wouldn't let me finish my questions, the only one of our suspects to take that attitude. Which argued—to my mind anyway—that he couldn't be guilty if he wasn't sufficiently interested to find out what I wanted to know. There was also, of course, the impression I got when I talked to Reade myself, but that isn't evidence either.'

'Even if he was threatened,' said Roger slowly, 'I can see he'd be afraid for Irene and the children, but damn it all, I'd have given him a key if he'd told me.'

'That probably never occurred to him.'

'Well, I can see we'll have to dissolve the partnership ... don't you think?' said Roger, unconsciously using one of Antony's favourite phrases. 'But I can't help being glad the police won't come into it. I mean, it would have hurt Irene frightfully.' He looked at Meg for a moment, and then smiled and turned to Sir Nicholas with what seemed like genuine amusement. 'I suppose you think that's all very reprehensible, Uncle Nick.'

Sir Nicholas was not to be drawn. 'It is only what I might have expected,' he said austerely. 'Of any of you,' he added deliberately, taking time to look from one to other of his audience, daring them to remind him that he was being inconsistent. 'This disregard for law and order—'

Things were getting back to normal. It was only Antony who wondered what his uncle's reaction would be after he'd seen the newspapers on Monday morning. Jenny's ingenuity was probably equal to seeing that the more lurid journals were suppressed, but even the ones he usually saw would carry some version of the story. The trouble was, Meg Hamilton was news.